The

Classic Crime

Library

#19

BY LAWRENCE BLOCK

NOVELS:

A Diet Of Treacle • After The First Death • Ariel • Campus Tramp • Cinderella Sims • Coward's Kiss • Deadly Honeymoon • The Girl With The Long Green Heart • Grifter's Game • Killing Castro • Lucky At Cards • Not Comin' Home To You • Random Walk • Ronald Rabbit Is A Dirty Old Man • Small Town • The Specialists • Such Men Are Dangerous • The Triumph Of Evil • You Could Call It Murder • The Girl With The Deep Blue Eyes

COLLECTED SHORT STORIES:

Sometimes They Bite • Like A Lamb To Slaughter • Some Days You Get The Bear • One Night Stands And Lost Weekends • Enough Rope • Catch And Release • Defender Of The Innocent

THE MATTHEW SCUDDER NOVELS:

The Sins Of The Fathers • Time To Murder And Create • In The Midst Of Death • A Stab In The Dark • Eight Million Ways To Die • When The Sacred Ginmill Closes • Out On The Cutting Edge • A Ticket To The Boneyard • A Dance At The Slaughterhouse • A Walk Among The Tombstones • The Devil Knows You're Dead • A Long Line Of Dead Men • Even The Wicked • Everybody Dies • Hope To Die • All The Flowers Are Dying • A Drop Of The Hard Stuff • The Night And The Music

THE BERNIE RHODENBARR MYSTERIES:

Burglars Can't Be Choosers • The Burglar In The Closet • The Burglar Who Liked To Quote Kipling • The Burglar Who Studied Spinoza • The Burglar Who Painted Like Mondrian • The Burglar Who Traded Ted Williams • The Burglar Who Thought He Was Bogart • The Burglar In The Library • The Burglar In The Rye • The Burglar On The Prowl • The Burglar Who Counted the Spoons

FOUR LIVES
AT THE CROSSROADS

Lawrence Block

A LAWRENCE BLOCK PRODUCTION

The Classic Crime Library

*Available in paperback from Hard Case Crime

Chapter 1

There are the big cities, where the teenage boys line up on feeble-minded jailbait in cellar clubs, where the gays cruise in drag and the dykes wear the pants. There are the suburbs, where all the houses look alike and all the people look alike and everybody, sooner or later, knocks off a piece with everybody else's wife. There are the farms, where they diddle the milkmaids in haylofts, and there are the port towns, where they screw the shopgirls on the piers, and there are the army towns, where they nail the camp followers on Saturday night after the paychecks have been dispersed.

There are also the villages, the warm-hearted home towns of Small-Town America fresh from the latest Norman Rockwell cover. The village is town meetings and cracker-barrel philosophy and the general store and rosy-cheeked girls and freckle-faced boys and old men and women who sit on porches in rocking chairs, chewing and spitting and listening to the sound of their arteries hardening. The village may also be a lynch mob hanging a baffled black man from a convenient tree limb, or a red-necked justice of the peace fining out-of-state motorists for driving twenty miles an hour in a twenty-five-mile-an-hour zone, or a pregnant and unmarried girl being shamed and shunned and ridden out of town on a rail. Hey, you have to take the bad with the good, and the village is what made America the great nation she is today. You got a problem with that?

Cedar Corners was a village. Specifically, Cedar Corners was a village in Indiana, a hamlet of forty-five hundred souls in relative degrees of purity. It was situated on the banks of the Rinasaukee River, a stream that froze up in winter and dried up in summer and trickled aimlessly during the remaining two seasons of spring and fall. No cedar trees grew in Cedar Corners. There were corners, however—the usual complement of four per city block. No one was quite sure how the village had been named, but the name was a fairly simple one, easy to pronounce and easy to remember. One Jeremiah Lumpsnell had founded the town ages back for lack of anything else to do, and some fifteen years ago his sole surviving descendant, an old-maid schoolteacher named Hephzibah Lumpsnell, had pressed the city fathers to change the town's name from Cedar Corners to Lumpsnell.

This had not happened. The name of the town remained Cedar Corners, and, with the subsequent and by no means premature death of Hephzibah Lumpsnell, any threat to the name had disappeared forever.

Nothing much ever happened in Cedar Corners. Every

couple of years the town gave from eighty to ninety percent of its votes to whatever Republican was running for something. Every now and then a baby was born, and every now and then a couple was married, either of its own free will or because it was expecting offspring. Every now and then the brighter youths fled the town and ran off to New York and Chicago, and every now and then a married couple was divorced, and every now and then someone died and was buried in the cheerless cemetery across Winding Hill Road.

All in all, Cedars Corners was a pleasant place to live, unexciting but not quite deadly. There was no racial problem, because the seventeen Negroes who lived in the town were not manifestly discontent with their lot. There was no problem of anti-Semitism, because the town's one Jew, a sallow-faced man named Milton Aaronson, was that indispensable sort of doctor who made house calls willingly at any hour, who charged very low rates, and who never pressed for payment. Since Dr. Aaronson had even less desire to join the Cedar Corners Country Club than the members had to have him, there was little friction.

If the summer had not been abnormally hot one year, and if four persons in particular had not been residing in Cedar Corners at that particular time, it is possible that nothing of note would ever have occurred in Cedar Corners. But the summer *was* hot, and Cedar Corners was blessed (or damned, as you prefer it) with these four persons. They were Betty Marie James, Luke Penner, Joyce Ramsdell, and Martin McLeod.

*   *   *

Betty Marie James was taking off her blouse.

This could have been more interesting than it was. She could have been taking off her blouse in a smoke-filled room while a crowd of intoxicated Legionnaires cheered her on. Or she could have been taking off her blouse in the back seat of a three-year-old Ford while a youthful swain panted feverishly, his hands itching for her breasts. This, sad to say, was not the case. She was in her own room in her parents' house on Willow Lane, and she was alone, and there is nothing remarkably devilish about a girl removing her blouse under such circumstances.

Still, it was noteworthy. If just any girl had been performing the same act, one might dismiss it with a verbal shrug and move on to something else. But Betty Marie James, especially without a blouse, was spectacular.

She was sixteen years old. A look at her face let you believe her age, whereas you might be inclined to doubt it if you only looked at her body. Her blonde hair was long and fluffy, falling down over her shoulders in golden waves. Her eyes were cornflower blue and quite large; you might have called them innocent eyes if you didn't notice the set to them and the lines of tension at their corners. Her mouth was full, her lips red even without lipstick. She had a firm pointed chin and a broad, bright forehead.

The body took up where the face left off. The body had the approximate shape of an hourglass, but when you looked at that body you forgot what time it was. Her waist was an isthmus connecting two larger bodies of land. Her hips were full, and her buttocks were substantial, and her thighs were taut and sensual, tapering to well-turned calves and trim ankles and feet. Above the waist—and this is the part that showed when the blouse we have been discussing came off—above the waist, Betty Marie James was pretty spectacular.

Her breasts were not the breasts of a sixteen-year-old girl. They were the breasts of a woman. They were very large and had been large for several years; boys in her class at Cedar Corners High had referred to her privately as Titty Marie James for some time. They were firm as a hard-shell Baptist on the existence of God, and they came to points as prominent as a pregnant nun, and those points were as red as arterial blood.

Betty Marie was studying her breasts in the mirror. She was tired, and she was bored, and it was hot as hell out, and she was stuck in her room with nothing for company but her breasts. She put a hand beneath each breast, lifted them slightly in her palms, and observed all this action very dispassionately in the mirror. She noted the weight of her breasts, and the satin softness of the skin on their undersides, and she smiled at her mirror image.

Luke Penner liked those breasts, she thought. Luke Penner damn near dampened his drawers every time he got a hand on one of them, and he got a hand on one every chance he had. She remembered the last time, just a night ago, with his hands flexing her breasts and pinching her nipples until she thought she was going to lose her mind. Luke Penner, when you came right down to it, was pretty goddamned nuts about those breasts.

Luke Penner was pretty goddamned nuts about everything that concerned Betty Marie, as far as that went. He wanted to go out with her whenever he possibly could, and he wanted to park in his three-year-old Ford and neck with her at the conclusion of each date, and he wanted to marry her.

The guy had it all planned out. In a year he would graduate from high school, and she would drop out, and they would be married. A year or so after that they would have a baby before the army got around to calling him up, and they would have more babies over the years, and Luke would run his father's gas station and take it over when Cray Penner died, and that would be that.

This would have been far more appealing if Betty Marie were pretty goddamned nuts about Luke Penner.

She wasn't.

Not at all.

She released her breasts, peeled down her dungarees, got out of them, shucked her underpants, ran her hands briefly over her body, then threw herself face down on the bed. Damn, she thought. She didn't want to spend the rest of her life in Cedar Corners, didn't want to be picking up after a passel of brats before she was twenty years old. She was young, and she wanted to do a little living before it was time to die.

Being married to Luke Penner wasn't living. It might be fine for plenty of girls, but for Betty Marie it would just be a quiet and painless way to die young. She wanted more than that. She wanted excitement, a fast ride on a hot merry-go-round with plenty of brass rings to reach for. You didn't find that kind of excitement in Cedar Corners. You had to get up and get out, go someplace like Chicago or Los Angeles where things were happening.

She had been tempted to leave. That was the easy way—pack up and ship out, just go somewhere and see what would happen. But it didn't always work out. She knew about Lucy Mackie, a girl a few years older than Betty Marie. Lucy had run off with a salesman who had spent a few days in Cedar Corners, and nobody heard anything from her for months, and then one day she was back in town again living at home, and her belly was swollen up. They said she had married the salesman and then divorced him, but that was just a convenient lie and nobody even pretended to believe it.

Betty Marie shivered. That wasn't the way she wanted it. You couldn't come home pregnant and dragging your tail between your legs. You couldn't make yourself something for the whole town to snicker at. But you couldn't just stick around and die a little at a time, either. There had to be some way to escape, some safe way. But she didn't know what it was.

She sighed. Luke was coming that night, coming to take her out again. Maybe he'd try to make her go all the way. Well, maybe she would let him do what he wanted.

At least it would be something different.

*   *   *

Martin McLeod sat at a stool in the Corners Tavern and smoked a cigarette while he drank straight bourbon from a water tumbler. There was an order to his actions; he would first take a sip of whiskey, then a puff of the cigarette, and finally a breath of air. The whiskey was fair to good, the cigarette was like any cigarette, and the air was stale. In the Corners Tavern, the air was always stale.

If you were a man who liked to drink, and if you lived in Cedar Corners, you did not have much choice. You could drive to Harrisport and pick up a bottle at the state liquor store, or you could do your drinking at the Corners Tavern. It was the only bar in Cedar Corners. The Land's End Cafe sold bottled beer with meals, but the tavern was the only place in town where you could get hard liquor.

Marty McLeod liked hard liquor. He liked the taste of it, and he liked the warm glow it gave you as it went down your throat straight with no chaser. And he liked the feeling that came when you had enough of it in your system. Not the drunk feeling, because only a fool drank himself blind. The loose feeling, the easy feeling. Some people were lucky—they could get that feeling just by taking things easy. The only time Marty McLeod could take things easy was when he had enough alcohol in his bloodstream.

He hadn't yet reached that state, and his glass was now empty. He held it a few inches above the bar top, and the bartender came over and tilted the bottle to pour more bourbon into it. The bartender was named Dan and he owned the place. He never swept the floor and he never opened a window, but he poured big drinks and kept the prices down.

"You're a good customer," he said, "but you keep me busy. Wasn't for you, I could sleep till after dinner."

Marty looked around. He was the only customer in the bar.

"People don't drink much in the afternoon. You better watch out, boy. People be talking about you."

"People always talk about me."

"Yeah?"

"Yeah," Marty said. "Ever since I stuck a knife in that fucker over in Greeley, people never've stopped talking about me. It grates on you, after a while."

The bartender looked at him for a moment, oddly. Then he made himself remember something he had to do at the other end of the bar. He went away and McLeod lit another cigarette from the butt of the one he had been smoking. He took a drink of the bourbon, set the glass down, blew out a cloud of smoke.

Ever since I stuck a knife in the fucker over in Greeley . . .

He remembered it clearly enough. It wasn't the sort of thing you'd forget easily. He'd been easy-going Marty McLeod then, the up-and-comer trying to make a go of it with a small-town law office, the guy with a pretty wife and a two-story white house at the edge of town with a lawn in front and a garden in back and a GI mortgage on the place.

Until he came home early one afternoon, and let himself in with his key, and walked up a flight of stairs, and went into the bedroom. And found his wife, nude, legs apart, a man kneeling between them.

The knife was one he had used before for scaling fish. He didn't remember picking it up, but he must have. The Medical Examiner told the court at the trial that he had counted thirty-seven stab wounds in the man's body. So he must have picked up the knife, and he must have done a number on the son of a bitch who had been on his knees, having lunch at the Y. Cut him enough to kill him several times over, but he didn't kill his wife, didn't even touch her. He just ignored the woman's screams while he stabbed the man until his arm ached. Then he went down to the police station and told them all about it.

They called it manslaughter, and they made it a quick and easy trial, with McLeod's attorney emphasizing the perverted nature of the act the dead man had been performing, and the inevitable impact of such an act upon his client's psyche. The prosecution didn't fight too hard, and the jury got the point, and in the end they gave him a year at McAllister Pen because they couldn't let him off with less than that. There was no getting around the fact that he'd killed a man, but considering what and with whom the man had been doing, well, what could you expect him to do? But they kept up appearances by giving him a year. He packed a suitcase and went to McAllister, and with time off for good behavior he was out in eight months.

But he didn't go back to Greeley. There was nothing there for him. When you have been convicted of a felony, you cannot practice law any more. He'd been a lawyer on the way up, and now he was just another ex–con, and even if they liked him in Greeley they would go on talking about him forever. He couldn't feel comfortable there, and all Greeley could do was remind him of the life he threw away when he picked up the knife. So he didn't go to Greeley. Instead he moved to Cedar Corners, and he was there now.

He drank more bourbon. He'd been in Cedar Corners for three months now. He owned a three-room shack on the edge of town, a little bungalow without basement or attic or garage that someone had thrown together as temporary housing after the war and that no one ever bothered to tear down. The house had cost him a thousand dollars, and the car he drove cost him another thousand. Living cost him very little. He had to buy food, and he had to buy gas for the car, and he had to buy booze and cigarettes. That was about it.

He drew on the cigarette, dragged more smoke down into his lungs. Living here three months, he thought, but you couldn't say he belonged yet. He wasn't a true resident of Cedar Corners. He was just someone who was living there for a spell, slinging hash from midnight to eight in the morning at the Land's End Cafe, sleeping mornings, drinking afternoons and evenings. And waiting. He was waiting for something, but he didn't know exactly what it was.

Waiting for something to happen, he thought. When it did, well, that was time enough to know what it was.

He knocked off the bourbon and motioned for a refill. Dan filled the glass again and went away without speaking. Good, he thought. The bastard talked too much anyway.

McLeod sipped the bourbon. According to his watch, it was a quarter to five. The watch was a ten-dollar bargain from an Indianapolis hockshop, with a sweat-stained wristband and a scratched crystal, but as long as he remembered to wind it, it kept perfect time.

He was supposed to meet Joyce at six. She was going to feed him dinner at her place, and then, if things went according to established tradition, he was going to fuck her until it was time to go to work at the Land's End Cafe. They would kill a bottle together, and they would work out her bedsprings together, and then he would go to work at the cafe.

He laughed. If you were just killing time, Joyce Ramsdell was the type of pig to kill it with. She wasn't bad to look at and she was dynamite in the rack, but she was a pig. A sloppy stupid bitch. A slut, a tramp. Loads of fun, and no chance you would fall in love with her because a man only loved one rotten whore in his life, and McLeod had already been married to his. Joyce was somebody to kill time with. But the day she started getting ideas about how nice it would be if he moved in, that was the day he would move out. Out of her life—and while he was at it, out of Cedar Corners.

He finished his drink and went out to the car. It was parked at the curb, an old Chevy with a do-it-yourself paint job that was beginning to rust through. The floorboards were slightly shot and the shock absorbers could have been replaced if he gave enough of a damn to invest additional money in the car. The engine was a good one and that was all he cared about. The car started when he turned the key, and it got him wherever he was going, and that was enough.

He settled himself behind the wheel, stuck the key in the ignition and gunned the motor. He drove bluntly, slamming the Chevy from one gear to another, braking hard, accelerating swiftly. He didn't do anything fancy. He was not a fancy person.

Thirty-four years old, and looking older. Hair so dark a brown that it was very nearly black. A chin like a boulder. Brown eyes, dark complexion. Tall, well past six feet. Big all over—wide shoulders, big arms, a barrel of a chest. He had never really looked much like a lawyer. Prison toughened him and broadened him, and now he looked less like a lawyer than ever. More like a stevedore, or a ditch-digger, or a maybe a muscleman for the mob. But when you spent more time looking at the eyes you realized he was smarter than you thought, so you weren't too sure just what he looked like. Like a lawyer, say, who did a year less good behavior time at McAllister at hard labor for killing a man with a knife. Something like that.

Back at his house, he carried out the garbage and stuffed it in a can at the side of the road. He straightened up the place to make it livable. He had kept a neat cell in the penitentiary and he kept a neat house at Cedar Corners. He couldn't live sloppy.

Not like Joyce. Jesus, she was a sloppy bitch!

*   *   *

It was a Friday, and the alimony check came in the afternoon mail the way it always did on Fridays. As usual, it was not alone. Along with it there was a mail-order catalog from a firm in Beverly Hills offering party records, a letter inviting a contribution to a fund designed to relieve the suffering of sharecroppers in the South, a batch of coupons which would entitle the bearer to discounts ranging from three cents to eight cents on various brands of soap powders, and a picture postcard of the Great Salt Lake.

Joyce looked at each piece of mail in turn. She tore up and discarded everything but the alimony check and the postcard. She read the message through three times. It was from somebody named Phil, and it said that Phil sure remembered the fine time they had had and hoped to see his little Joycie again right soon. She tried to remember Phil's last name, tried to conjure up an image of what he had looked like, and failed on both counts. She turned the postcard over and looked at the lake, deciding it didn't look particularly salty. She tore the postcard in half and threw it away.

The bank was still open when she got there. Each week she had to rush to get her alimony check to the bank on time, and each time she got there just under the wire. She cashed the check, took the money in fives and tens and crammed the bills into her purse. Then she hurried back to her house and made herself a cup of coffee.

Joyce Ramsdell. You couldn't say that she was pretty, but there was an animalistic erotic quality to her that made you stop caring whether she was pretty or not. Her mouth was a red wound, her hair was sin-black, her hips were comfortably ample, and her breasts were a more than adequate cushion for a man's chest. Her nose was too wide and her eyes were set a little too close together, and her chin was a little weak. She wasn't pretty, but she was hot.

Now, most women look hottest when they're nude, or when they're dressed up to look their best, or in a revealing negligee. Joyce was different. Right now she was wearing a shapeless housedress, and she had no makeup on, and there were dark circles around her eyes from too much bed and not enough sleep. And she could not possibly have looked sexier.

She was a special type of woman. She was all animal, and if you took one look at her you knew right off that she would do anything in the world and that she could go all night without losing her enthusiasm for it. There is a woman like Joyce Ramsdell in every town in the nation, a woman who wants nothing but a good time, a woman who has nothing to offer but the area from her navel to her knees and who consequently offers it to any and all.

A tramp, then. But not just any tramp. A tramp the whole town had the hots for.

She stirred her coffee, took a sip of it. It was too hot and she put the cup down again on the cluttered kitchen table. She patted her purse happily. A damn good thing about that alimony, she thought. A very damn good thing. What the hell would she do without that once-a-week check? Go nuts, probably. Starve. Or sell her rear end on a full-time basis like a common whore.

And let's be clear on this: she wasn't a whore. She gave it away pretty freely, admittedly, but she didn't charge for it. Once in a while a man might bring her a present, or slip her a few dollars and tell her to buy herself something nice. Or bring over two or three bottles of liquor and never have more than a single drink.

But that was as far as it went. She didn't sell it. If you sold it you were a whore, and she didn't want to be a whore, and the alimony let her live the sort of life she wanted to lead without being a whore. So she wasn't a whore—she was a tramp instead, and while the subtle distinction might have struck some souls as purely academic, it was important to her.

The coffee was cool enough to drink now. She sipped it and got a cigarette going. It was instant coffee and it didn't taste as good as regular coffee, but she hardly ever made regular coffee. It was too much trouble. For instant you just boiled some water and spooned some coffee into a cup and poured the water on the coffee and gave it a stir, and you were set. It was a lot easier and a lot faster, and she wasn't the type of woman who liked to fuss around a lot in the kitchen. She was a lot more at home in the bedroom.

She laughed suddenly. McLeod would be coming over pretty soon. She would throw some slop together and call it dinner, and once they got it out of the way they could belt the bottle around and then fall in bed together. Jesus, she loved it with McLeod. He was all man, top to bottom, from the skin to the bone. There was no time wasted with

McLeod. He was a tough son of a bitch, and that was the way she wanted her man to be. Tough.

The first time with McLeod: she had picked him up at the tavern, where he had been drinking for five hours. He wasn't drunk. She picked him up bold as brass, just walked over to the stool where he was sitting and draped an arm around his shoulder and stuck her tongue in his ear. Not subtle, not subtle at all. Pretty damn direct and to the point.

He hadn't been subtle either. He turned around slowly, let his eyes go from her face to her feet and back again. He reached out a hand and tweaked her nipple right there with everybody watching. He was that kind of man; he just didn't give a damn what anybody thought.

"Hot as a stove," he had said.

"So?"

"Come on," he said. "Let's find a bed."

They had found a bed. Her bed, in her house—the house Jack Ramsdell had left her when he got sick and tired of finding her in bed with other men. They found it, and they used it, and he sent her to the moon and back again.

When she was with McLeod she didn't need other men. When she was with McLeod she didn't need anything but the hard toughness of him driving at her, punishing her, fulfilling her. McLeod was all she needed. She never said anything about this to him, but since they first made love seven or eight weeks ago she had not given herself to another man. Only McLeod.

She sipped her coffee and smiled.

*　　　*　　　*

Luke Penner rolled a cigarette. He held a piece of cigarette paper in his left hand between thumb and forefinger, and he poured Bull Durham from a cotton sack into the depression in the paper. The first cigarette didn't turn out too well, all lopsided and flimsy, and he threw it away and tried again. The second came out better, and he twisted the ends, scratched a match and smoked.

He was seventeen with sandy hair and prominent front teeth, tall and lanky and unfinished in appearance. He played fair basketball and he ran the hundred in ten seconds flat with a good tailwind. In a year he would graduate from high school. In a year he would begin working full-time at his father's Texaco station at the intersection of Route 174 and River Hill Road. In a year he would marry Betty Marie James.

His handmade cigarette was beginning to come apart in his fingers. He dropped it to the ground, stepped on it. He was happy. He picked up the basketball, drove in toward the basket over the garage door, sank an easy lay-up. But it was too hot to fool around with a basketball. He tossed it into the garage and went into the house.

His mother was getting dinner ready. A faded woman, old already and not yet forty. She had had four children that lived and two that didn't, and that takes a lot out of a person.

"Dinner'll be ready in a few minutes," she told him. "Better get washed up."

"Sure," he said. "What are we having?"

"Pot roast and mashed potatoes. Good enough for you?"

He grinned at her. "Better feed me good," he said. "I got a date tonight."

"With Betty Marie?"

She always asked. He had been dating Betty Marie and nobody but Betty Marie for more than a year now, and she always asked. "That's right," he said. "Betty Marie."

"Pretty girl, Luke."

"She sure is."

"You figure on getting settled right off the bat," she said gently. "Just get married and settle down and raise a family. That right?"

"That's right."

She studied her hands. "Well," she said. "You know, sometimes a boy wants to kick up his heels first, get out in the world and have a time for himself afore he settles down. You got to settle down *from* something, you know."

He didn't say anything.

"Sometimes a boy's got a lot of growing to do afore he's a man."

"I've done a lot of growing, Ma. I'm pretty tall, aren't I?"

"Not what I mean."

"No?" He looked at her. "I don't get it," he said.

She shrugged.

"I love Betty Marie," he said. "I want to marry her. I'm ready to settle myself down, ready to work hard and make a good life. You like it better if I was some kind of a hell-raiser, Ma?"

"I didn't say that."

"Then—"

"You better wash up," she said. "Dinner'll be ready any minute now and you better be ready if you got a date tonight."

Dinner was good, as usual, and he ate heartily. Afterward he went outside and sat on the lawn chair in the yard smoking another handmade cigarette and letting his dinner settle. His sister Alice, the older of the two girls, was primping in the bathroom. Timmy and Gwen were watching television. His Dad was on his way back to the Texaco station and his mother was doing the dishes.

And he was thinking about what his mother had said. Heck, he thought, you'd think she'd be glad to see he had both feet on the ground. Other kids, they didn't know *what* they wanted to do with themselves. Jimmy Kell, now, he was fixing to do his three years in the army and then see what turned up. George Ryan was going to try college for a while, but Luke knew he wouldn't stick it out. They were required to take every kid in the state with a high school diploma at the University, but they didn't have to keep you if you couldn't stick it, and most of the freshman class busted out after the first semester. George wouldn't be there long.

Eddie and Loco were just going to hang around, maybe hunt up jobs. Bill was always talking about heading for California or Alaska, but Luke figured it was just talk, and he was about as likely to go to China, or the moon. Jesus, he thought, how could they live lives with no plan? How could they do it?

He shook his head, clucked his tongue. Well, that was the difference between him and the rest of them. And maybe Betty Marie was a big part of that difference. When you had a girl like Betty Marie, well, you had something worth settling down with. Sweet and pretty, fun to be with, nice to talk to, and when you kissed her it made your head go around in circles. He didn't know if she could cook, but she could learn, and he knew for sure she'd be a perfect mother, and when they were married she would sleep with him every night and it would be like going to heaven, but without dying first.

He clucked his tongue again. If they weren't careful, though, it was going to be tough waiting until they were married. He was just crazy about her, and when they necked in their special parking place sometimes he almost lost his head. And she never tried to stop him, either. She trusted him all the way, and it was rough on a guy when a girl trusted him that much. He had to control himself, and with a girl like Betty Marie it was tough to keep that control in place.

Sometimes he even thought she wanted to go all the way, and it worried him. But he knew they would manage to wait, to make it last until they were married. And then it would be better. Otherwise it would be a little like opening your Christmas presents a week early. You got the thrill of opening them, and that was exciting and all, but what fun was it when Christmas came and you didn't have any presents to open?

His mind played with the idea of Betty Marie all

gift-wrapped, and unwrapping her, and her body opening to him, her mouth open, her legs parted—

Whoa!

He let out a low whistle, then jumped to his feet and raced back into the house. He had to hurry, had to wash up, had to take himself a quick shave. He could get by without a shave, but he always felt better if he shaved before he went out on a date with Betty Marie. Even if he didn't need to.

Chapter 2

Start on Main Street two blocks up from the river. That puts you at the corner of Main and Limestone. Now walk four blocks farther on Main until you get to Walker Street. That four-block stretch is what a resident of Cedar Corners means when he says *Downtown.* And those four blocks contain pretty much everything Cedar Corners has to offer. There's the State, open seven nights a week to show westerns and war movies. The Land's End Cafe serves fair food, bottled beer, and canned music from a rusty juke for occasional dancing. There are two drugstores in the four-block stretch, and one gas station, and a supermarket, and a hardware store, and a used-car showroom, and a dry goods store. The Corners Tavern is there. The general stores—there are two of them, and the owners hate one another almost as much as they both hate the twentieth century—are also there. This is Main Street, downtown Main Street, in Cedar Corners.

Limestone Street, cutting east and west at the foot of Downtown, plays Forty-Second Street to Main Street's Broadway. The cheaper stores and eateries are to be found on Limestone on either side of Main, and the cheaper people hang out there. There is a barber shop, and the man with the scissors sells numbers tickets and handles the Cedar Corners horse betting, what there is of it. He also cuts hair, because you can't retire on what Cedar Corners drops at the track. There is a beauty parlor, a laundry or two, a second-hand furniture store, a food shop or three, and another used-car lot.

The difference between Limestone Street and Main Street, from a standpoint of social utility, may be illustrated thusly. When a Cedar Corners boy is out on a date with a girl whom he likes and respects, he may take her for a bite at the Land's End, or to some other Main Street spot. When he is out with another girl and is taking her out solely in the expectation of getting in her pants, he will buy her a hamburger at Big John's on Limestone Street, or a soda at the Green Dragon Malt Shoppe. While Limestone Street is certainly not a shady place, it is second-rate.

McLeod was on Limestone Street. He had dropped into the barbershop for a shine, and while the colored kid was working on his shoes and whistling "Chattanooga Shoeshine Boy" a man named Burl sidled over to him. McLeod wasn't sure whether Burl was the man's first or last name. No one ever called him anything else.

"Marty," Burl said. "How you fixed for dough?"

"I got none to spare."

Burl chuckled, and all of his chins shook. He put a hand on McLeod's shoulder and McLeod didn't shrink away. In McAllister Pen they taught you not to cringe no matter who touched you.

"I don't mean lending," Burl said. "I mean getting some."

"How?"

Burl hawked and spat. There was a brass spittoon on the floor and he missed it. He wiped his mouth with the back of one hand, then wiped the hand on his baggy pants. The spit sat on the floor and reflected light.

"You can use money?"

"I can always use money."

"This is easy money, McLeod."

"It always is."

Burl chuckled again. An unpleasant sound, McLeod thought. A sloppy fat man with a bad smell to him.

"But real easy," Burl said. "Rolling off a log—that easy. The money is there waiting for somebody to get hungry. You hungry, McLeod?"

"I could probably work up an appetite."

"Me, I'm always hungry," Burl said. "Fact is I could do with something to eat right now. I'll be at Big John's. We can talk there."

The colored kid finished the shine and McLeod tossed him a half a buck and told him to put the change toward a Cadillac. The kid popped the shoeshine rag, flipped the half-dollar into the air, caught it and pocketed it. McLeod left the barber shop, stopped in the doorway to light a cigarette.

People didn't have to be told you were an ex-con, he thought. The people who knew anything at all could smell it on you. After a year at McAllister you didn't come up smelling like a rose. And the men with the beautiful ideas always found you. There was the guy he'd shared a cell with, a hardheaded mug named Gray, with a bank set-up that you could crack like an egg with a four-man operation. Gray talked that bank night and day for eight months. He was still in the jug and he was probably still talking.

McLeod looked at his watch. It was time to run over to Joyce's and throw her a quickie to keep her happy. But he didn't much feel like it. He was more interested in learning what Burl was talking about.

He found a phone and dropped a dime, dialed Joyce's number. She answered on the third ring.

"Marty," he said.

"Soup's on, Marty. Get over here."

"Keep the soup warm," he told her.

"What's the matter?"

"I'll be a few minutes late."

"Yeah?"

"Yeah. I ran into a guy."

"With the car?"

He thought it was a bad joke, then realized she was serious. "No," he said. "Not with the car. With a locomotive. I'll be over when I can."

She wasn't particularly happy but he didn't particularly care. Keep the soup warm, he thought. Keep the aspidistra flying. He knew where she could put the soup if she wanted to keep it warm.

He threw his cigarette in the gutter and walked half a block to Big John's. The place was a diner and Big John was a fat Greek with glossy black hair and wide shoulders.

Burl was in a booth at the back. There were no waitresses at Big John's. McLeod picked up a mug of black coffee at the counter and carried it to the booth. He sat down, put a spoon in his coffee to make it cool quickly.

Did that even work? He didn't figure it made much of a difference. His father had always done it, explaining that the metal spoon conducted the heat away from the liquid. It had sounded plausible, but the old man had said no end of things over the years, and most of them turned out to be horseshit. Still, McLeod did as he'd done out of habit. He didn't see that it could do any harm, and that put it out in front of all the rest of his habits.

"All right," he said. "Let's hear it."

"You'll like this, Marty."

"Sure."

Burl was eating apple pie. He had a glass of milk at his elbow. He stuffed a forkful of pie into his big mouth and washed it down with milk. He grinned.

"Let's go, Burl."

"Good pie," Burl said.

"The pitch, Burl."

"Yeah," the fat man said. "Marty, you'll like this."

First they went to the State. The movie, as usual, was a western. It was entitled *The Sound of Distant Tom-Toms,* and it was billed as an adult western because it ended with the hero kissing his girlfriend instead of his horse. It was accompanied by three cartoons, a newsreel, and a trailer promoting next week's western.

It was about what you'd expect.

Betty Marie put up with it because there was nothing else to do. The picture had its moments, too; there was one scene where Alan Ladd beat hell out of the madam of a whorehouse—although in the film they pretended that it was just a dancehall, since it wasn't that adult a western. He slammed her in the stomach, punched her in the eye, and kicked her in the side when she fell on the floor. Betty Marie liked that. She thought it was somewhat out of character for a natural-born straight shooter like Alan Ladd, but she liked that kind of a scene.

She might have liked the picture itself more if it hadn't been so much a part of their routine. In all the time they had been going together, they had never missed a new movie at the State. It wasn't all Luke's fault either. True, he always suggested a movie. But she never rejected the idea, because, when you came right down to it, what else was there to do?

Not much.

Nothing, really.

And that, in the shell of a nut, was the story of the hotsy-totsy life she could look forward to if she followed the easy road and married Luke Penner. It would be a life of nothing much, a life of catching every new bill at the State and watching Alan Ladd and Randolph Scott and John Wayne take care of fresh bad men each week. They would do other things, of course, just as they did other things now.

But the movies were what they always did, and would always do, world without end, amen.

After the show they walked outside and stood for a moment on the sidewalk. The crowd poured out of the State. Wonderful, Betty Marie thought. Close your eyes and it's as though you were on Broadway. Wonderful.

"Want to get a soda?"

She looked at him. "Where?"

"Land's End, I guess."

Forty kids at once in the Land's End Cafe, with that new waiter Marty hopping to get all the orders right, and the juke blaring and the boys drinking beer and the girls drinking sodas and the same people everywhere.

"I don't want a soda," she said.

"How come?"

She looked at her wristwatch. "It's only ten o'clock," she said.

"So?"

"I just remembered. That waiter Marty doesn't come on until midnight. What's the point of going there now?"

He was baffled. "What difference does it make who pours a soda for you?"

"I've got hot pants for Marty. Didn't you know?"

The expression seemed to jar him a little. On top of that, he didn't seem sure that she was kidding. She laughed and took his arm. "Sorry," she said. "I've been in a funny mood all night. Let's drive down by the river and neck."

So, after not very much ado about anything or nothing, they drove down by the river. Summer had already taken care of the river, but they parked near where the river would have been if there had been any river at the time, and he killed the motor and engaged the emergency brake and reached for her, and she went to him at once. He kissed her mouth, familiar and warm and tasting just right, and it wasn't a bore any longer. It was fine, she was where she belonged, and everything was as it should be.

She kissed him with a passion that was almost fierce, as much to compensate for her earlier doubts as anything else. She had her arms tight around him, her breasts snuggling against his chest and her tongue tasting the familiarity of his mouth, and she put everything inside her into that kiss.

For five minutes—or ten minutes, or fifteen minutes— it went on like that. Mouths together, kissing, tongues moving softly and expertly. When two people went out to- gether for a sizable length of time, and when they conclud- ed each date with a necking session, it was to be expected that they would attain a degree of expertise as far as kissing one another was concerned. This had happened. Betty Ma- rie knew just how Luke kissed, and Luke knew just how Betty Marie kissed, and they both knew how the game was played.

Then, midway through a kiss, his hand moved as it al- ways did to cup her breast. She felt his fingers around the mound of taut flesh, simply holding her for a moment, holding her gently and tenderly. Then the fingers flexed and relaxed, flexed and relaxed, alternately squeezing and releasing the breast. Passion began to build within her body. She felt her heart beating faster, felt desire rising in

her system. She moaned—softly, almost imperceptibly—
and she pressed tighter against him.

His hand.

Holding her.

And then they were not kissing at all, and she was un-
doing the buttons of his shirt and running hot little hands
over his hairless chest, and he was opening her blouse and
tugging it free of her skirt and slipping it back over her
shoulders and letting it drop. She got her hands out of the
sleeves and threw her arms around him, hugging him.

"The bra," she whispered urgently. "Take off that damn
bra."

Usually there was an interval of love play between the
removal of the blouse and the subsequent removal of the
bra. But she was breaking that pattern tonight. She didn't
want to wait. Desire was stronger tonight, desperately
strong, and she didn't want to play the game according to
the usual body of rules.

He was a little awkward getting the bra off. There was a
hook-and-eye arrangement, and he had never managed to
get used to it. She could see how it might be a little tricky
the first time, but by now he'd taken off her bra almost as
many times as she'd put it on, and he still hadn't managed to
get the hang of it. He got it off eventually and put it aside,
and then her bare breasts leapt into his hands.

It was torture. He stroked them, kissed them, cupped
them, squeezed them, pinched their nipples, rolled the
hard rubies between his fingers until she wanted to shriek
with torment. Usually a little part of herself was always held

in reserve, sort of looking over one shoulder to keep on eye on her. Now the reserves had been called up to the front lines and all the protective measures were useless. She was hot as a steam room in July, hot as Chicago during the fire. She was trembling, and deep within herself she felt new fires igniting and new passions coming into existence.

Her hips churned involuntarily, caught up in a new motion that came as natural as dancing the twist. She tossed her body like a seated burlesque dancer, grinding out obscenities in motion. He went on doing delicious things to her breasts and she thought she was going to go up in a sheet of flame.

"My skirt," she said.

He looked at her oddly.

"Put your hand under my skirt," she said.

She wasn't supposed to give the orders, his face told her. He in all his infinite wisdom was supposed to decide when she had been sufficiently stimulated so that he might with impunity touch her intimately. But evidently his decision-making facilities were a little numb tonight. She was hot as hell and he didn't seem to realize it, or if he realized it he wasn't being very quick to take advantage of the fact.

"Reach up my skirt," she said again. "Touch me, Luke. Touch me."

This time he got the message. He was holding one breast and kissing the other, all of which left one hand free. The free hand settled on her knee, then moved along the inside of her thigh beneath the thin fabric of her skirt. The hand moved slowly—as far as she was concerned, he should just reach right for her at the start and grab her where she lived. It took a little time while he inched his way north, but finally he was there and she could feel his fingers through the sheer panties.

She was wet before he touched her, wetter still the minute she felt his fingers through the fabric. She squirmed and wriggled, moaned and panted. She wanted him, wanted him all the way, wanted him deep inside her, wanted to make the whole earth rock and roll with passion.

"The panties. Take them off."

He had never done this before. He did it now, and his hand returned and there was nothing in the way and he was touching her, probing her tentatively with tentative fingers, stroking, touching, fondling, driving her mad.

Take the fingers away, she wanted to yell. Put something else there. Come on, hurry up, let's have a happy. Come on, damn you—

She was reaching for him. She had touched him before, twice had caressed him until he gave a desperate little cry and jumped like a bomb. But she didn't want that now. No more kid stuff, dammit. No more games. Betty Marie James wanted to get her ashes hauled.

Too bad. Wasn't gonna happen.

Because first there was a moment, while she was still trying to take hold of him, when he stiffened and shook. And then he was pulling away, letting go of her, moving away from her and she was all alone by herself trying to clamp a lid on a body full of passions. She was burning up inside and he was leaving her alone and she thought she was going to die.

And, afterward, when the coolness came on in a way, he was smiling foolishly at her. "We almost got carried away," he said. "God, we must love each other a lot!"

That didn't seem to be the word for it, but she let it pass. She didn't trust herself to speak.

"It's good I was able to get hold of myself," he said. "Good I could control myself, Betty Marie."

"Control yourself? How, by coming in your pants?"

His eyes widened and she saw her words had shocked him. She wondered how he would play it, what he'd say, and discovered that his response was to suppress any reaction. She could see the wheels turn in his mind: A. A nice girl wouldn't say anything like that. B. She was a nice girl. C. Therefore she hadn't said it. D. Which meant he hadn't heard it. Which meant—

Which meant, she supposed, that he was controlling himself even more, which made him the most manly thing on earth since Steve Reeves played Hercules. Although she saw it a little differently; she saw an immature jerk who managed to cheat both of them out of a good time.

Control? She was the one who controlled herself. She didn't yell at him, and she didn't fight with him, and she didn't tell him what she thought of him. She simply asked him to take her home. He pointed out that it was only a few minutes after eleven. She told him something about how under the circumstances she'd better get home right away, before they really lost control. It was tough fitting her mouth around a sentence like that, but she managed it and it went over big. He grinned mannishly, roguishly, and started the car.

Just a few minutes after eleven—for Christ's sake, where did he expect to take her now? Her panties were sopping. If she walked into the Land's End they'd be able to smell her the minute she walked through the door.

Jesus . . .

He drove her home, and they went through the old goodnight-kiss-at-the-door-routine. The ritual had grown staler each time and now seemed ridiculous, given the circumstances. But she played her part, and then he was on his way back to the car, and she was in the house and heading up the stairs, and her damn fool mother was asking her if she had a good time.

"Of course," she cooed. "I always have a good time with Luke, Ma."

"You're not drinking," Joyce said.

She watched McLeod carefully. He had his pants on, his shirt and shoes off. He was sitting on the edge of the bed and he didn't say anything. She decided that he hadn't heard her.

"You're not drinking," she said.

"I heard you."

"Well?"

He shrugged.

"A card-carrying alcoholic like you," she said. "A boozehound like Marty McLeod. Since when aren't you drinking?"

"Forget it, Joyce."

She shut up. Actually he had had a few drinks since he'd come, but it wasn't the way it usually was. Usually he put a real dent in the bottle, and usually he put a dent in her, too, giving her the kind of workout that left her limp, and even a little sore.

Tonight was different. Tonight he hadn't shown until a few minutes after eight. And tonight he'd just had a couple of short drinks, and he had made love to her quickly and dispassionately, with his mind somewhere else. Had he even come? She didn't think he had, suspected he'd just gone through the motions until he'd decided it was time to stop.

Did men fake orgasms? She knew women did, and understood that some did so all the time. She'd pretended to come a couple of times over the years, but usually there was no need, because she could just about always reach orgasm.

God knows she always got there with McLeod.

But she could feel it now, could feel some weird tension in the air. She was not sure what it was all about but she didn't like it.

She said, "You can tell me about it, Marty."

He looked at her.

"Whatever it is," she said, "whatever's bugging you, you can tell me. I'm good at listening."

"Forget it," he said. "Just a mood."

"I'd say it's quite a mood."

"I just told you to forget it," he said. "So get the hell off my back, will you?"

The words were harsh but the tone was empty, emotionless. She sat still and put her hand to her face as though he had slapped her and she wanted to try rubbing the pain away. Then she picked up the bottle and drank a couple of ounces straight from it, just tilted the bottle up and let the liquor run down her throat. She put it down then, coughed, and smiled what was supposed to be seductive smile. McLeod didn't return the smile.

"It's getting late," he said.

"It's early."

"Late," he said. "Close to twelve. I got to get clothes on and get out of here. I'll be late for my shift."

She tried the smile again.

"There's time," she said.

"No, I better—"

She made an O of her mouth, extended her tongue, ran it around the circle of her lips. He could hardly miss the invitation in the gesture, but just shook his head.

"Not now. I'd better get going."

He was standing then, getting his shirt on, and she felt tears welling up somewhere behind her eyes. She stood up too and she grabbed at him, holding his arms. Her breasts were rising into his chest and he didn't seem to notice, or to care.

"Whatever I did," she said, "I'm sorry, Marty. Honest to God, I'm sorry."

"You didn't do anything."

"I didn't think I did. Look, what's up?"

"Nothing."

"Marty—"

But he drew away from her and put on his heavy black shoes one at a time, tied them in turn, tucked in his shirt, turned and headed for the door.

"Marty?"

"Listen," he said, "I'm in a mood. I'll see you tomorrow."

She heard the door slam. Then she sank slowly down on the bed. She did not have any clothes on. If she had been dressed she might have chased him out the door and run down the street after him, but her nudity was an effective brake on such behavior. She rolled over, buried her face in the fetid pillow, and drummed her feet in a rigid rhythm on the foot of the bed.

Damn, damn, damn!

He was her man, her only man, the only one she ever really got this hot over, the only one who was fun to be with and fun to drink with and fun to ball with and fun all across the board, the only one with guts inside and strength outside and everything a man had to have to keep a woman happy. And now he didn't want her any more. He didn't want her, he didn't care about her, he wouldn't even talk to her.

He didn't even want her to suck his cock.

She wanted to cry.

Men, she thought. Rotten, every last one of them.

Rotten filthy bastards. Rotten lousy stinking cruddy pigs. Men—

She finished the bottle. She picked it up, tilted it, opened her mouth and poured liquor down her throat, chugging it. Some of the liquor spilled and ran down her face, dripping onto her neck and her breasts. She slapped at her breasts to brush the liquor away and she hurt the soft flesh. She cursed, and she threw the empty bottle across the room. It hit the wall, bounced crazily, and finally broke into pieces.

Don't walk barefoot, she thought. You'll cut your feet to ribbons. Don't walk barefoot.

She stretched out on the bed, closed her eyes. She put her hands on her body, cupping breasts, examining loins, in an effort to assure herself that her body was still there, that it was still a good body, that there was nothing wrong with her that had made McLeod reject her. The breasts were large as ever, firm as ever. The body was taut and hungry as ever. There was nothing wrong with her, nothing that she could perceive.

She sighed. Then the liquor did its work and she closed her eyes and passed out.

Luke had to drive clear to Rushville to find the whore. He had dropped off Betty Marie at her house, then drove over to Land's End for a bottle of beer. A batch of the guys were there, some with dates and some without. He had two beers, paid up and left. Then he got in the car and started for Rushville, driving with the accelerator pedal close to the floorboards.

It was after two now, close to three, and he was in Rushville. He parked the car a block off the main drag and walked around for a few minutes to get the feel of the town. If you lived in Cedar Corners, he knew, and if you wanted to find a woman who would screw you for money, you went to Rushville. You hit a few of the downtown bars until you found a whore.

He had never gone there before. But the date with Betty Marie and the experience in the parked car had given him a need that had not been there before. He wanted to go all the way with a girl, with any girl. He wanted to do what he had to do, to feel what you were supposed to feel, to get his passport stamped and become a permanent exile from the miserable state of Virginity.

As it stood, it wasn't working out right. He knew, inside, that Betty Marie had wanted him to make love to her. The Christmas-present junk was all well and good, but the fact remained that she had wanted him and he had been too scared and too ignorant to do what he was supposed to do. Call it manly control all day long and it didn't change anything. He had crapped out.

He found the whore in a bar called Flaherty's on lower Main Street. The bar was loud and ugly and the jukebox gave out with country blues at top volume. He stood at the bar and ordered a beer. He drank it straight from the bottle and waited for something to happen.

It wasn't hard to see that the girl was a whore. She was

wearing too much makeup, and she was wearing an off-the-shoulders gown that let the tops of her breasts show, and she smiled all the time and she wiggled her ass when she walked. To remove any possible doubts, she sidled over to Luke, put her hand in his pants and asked him if he would like to have a party.

He was nervous. He covered it by turning to her and looking her up and down like an old whoremaster from way back, matching her smile with a tentative smile of his own. She still had her hand in his pants and she was holding onto him, all of which put him at a certain disadvantage, but he did his best.

"How much?" he asked.

"Ten bucks."

The whore would have taken five, and had been known to settle for a deuce, but Luke wasn't particularly adept at negotiating with prostitutes. He nodded nervously and she gave him another smile, then released him and freed her hand from his pants. She started for the door and he followed her. Outside he walked with her across Main and down a darker street toward her place.

"What a night," the whore said. "These slobs keep a girl busy, you know that?"

"Well," Luke said. "I can imagine."

"You better believe it. I had this one guy, one BJ wasn't enough for him. Once, twice, three times. Can you believe it? I thought my face was gonna fall off."

She stopped then, turned to him and kissed him. Her arms went around him and her mouth found his, and she wiggled against him for luck. Her tongue crept into his mouth and he thought of what she had done to the man, and what souvenirs he might have left in that rosebud mouth of hers, and he lost interest in the kiss.

The whore let go of him and they started walking again. She had a furnished room in a run-down clapboard building three blocks from Main Street. The building was not a whorehouse in that there was no madam and no parlor where prospective clients were received, but every room in the edifice was rented to a prostitute. The girls were model tenants. They paid high rentals, and they kept their rooms clean, and they didn't complain about noise.

Luke followed the whore to her room on the second floor. The room was small but neat. There was linoleum on the floor with a floral pattern. There was a picture of Jesus hung over the bed, and there was a lace doily on the dresser. The whore closed the door, bolted it, and took off her dress.

She had nothing on under the dress. Her breasts were small but perfectly formed, and her body was the taut and competent body of a hill girl. He had detected a note of Kentucky twang in her speech before, and he was excited. They said that the best whores in the country came from the Kentucky hills. Evidently he had picked a good one for his first time.

"Ten dollars," the whore said.

He found a ten-spot in his wallet and gave it to her. She checked the serial number—there had been a wave of counterfeits recently in that part of the country—then folded the bill once and put it in the top drawer of her dresser.

"Okay," she said. "Let's check you over."

He looked at her.

"Take your clothes off," she said.

She watched as he got undressed. Then she examined him. "Looks safe," she said. "But we better make sure, just in case."

Then she was opening a bottle, pouring a liquid into the palm of her hand, rubbing the liquid onto him. It was cold, and smelled like paint thinner.

"What's that?"

"Just alcohol," she said.

"What's it for?"

"Case you got a disease," she explained. "So as I won't get it. See?"

He saw. Then he let her draw him down onto the bed, and he kissed her, and he felt her small tight breasts touching him. He cupped a breast and gave it a squeeze. Smaller than Betty Marie's, he noticed, but nice.

"You can kiss 'em," she said. "If you want to."

He kissed her breasts, tongued them, nipped the nipples. He put one hand at her thigh and felt the sweet heat of her body. She took him in hand and held him, stroking him gently, and then she rolled him over onto his back, made him lie still, and crouched over him.

Her lips were softer than newly-fallen snow. Her tongue was hotter than molten lead. Her mouth did delicious things to him, dream things, and his body grew and swelled with passion and he was ready.

Quick as a wink she flopped over onto her back, bent

her legs at the knee, drew back each knee to open the path to paradise. He fell on her, and she guided him into place.

Then back and forth and up and down, and her piston-powered body bouncing him around, and his body thrusting spasmodically in and at her, filling her, sending showers of sparks over all the world.

Good.

Better . . .

Best!

The climax, when it came, was almost painful. The world exploded, and he filled her with the sweet smell of success, and it was over. He wanted to stay there forever, to spend the rest of his life between her thighs. But she rolled him away, got to her feet, hurried to the sink.

He watched her fill a basin with cold water. She squatted over the basin and splashed the water into herself and he watched, at once repelled and fascinated. "So I won't wind up with a baby," she said. "C'mere and I'll wash you off."

He almost said he wasn't worried about having a baby. But he let her wash him off, and felt himself beginning to respond to her touch, and wondered if he could afford another ten dollars, or if a second round might be less costly—but then she finished washing him and that was that. He got dressed and left her, and walked around until he found his car, and got into it, and drove off, headed back to Cedar Corners.

He was a man now.

Chapter 3

The crowd at the Land's End Cafe started to thin out at two when beer stopped being served. By three the place was down to a handful of regulars. By four most of the regulars were gone. A bald man sat at a stool reading an out-of-state newspaper while a cup of coffee cooled at his elbow. A long-haul trucker was putting away a mug of coffee and a wedge of apple pie. McLeod leaned against the counter, smoked a cigarette. In four hours he would be able to call it a night, go home, hit the sack.

He picked up a mug, drew himself black coffee from the nickel-plated urn, set the cup on the counter to cool. He wasn't tired but he was getting bored with the Land's End. He was glad the place was almost empty. There was next to nothing for him to do, and that way he had time to himself.

Time to think.

He was thinking about Burl, and about what Burl had told him. Burl had a plan. And the more McLeod thought about it the more he liked it. It was a good plan. It would probably work. If it worked, the payoff would be nice.

It was a simple plan. The best ones always were—he had

learned that much at McAllister and it was true enough. The involved, complicated plans always looked good at first, but the more complicated a plan was, the more things there were that could go wrong with it. His cell-mate, with his careful plan to crack that bank he never stopped talking about, didn't have much chance of pulling it off. Too many notions, all of which could fall apart. Too many cute little gimmicks that made good conversation after lights-out in the cell but that were guaranteed to bite you in the ass if you tried to pull them off. The good plans had to be simple.

In that respect, Burl's plan made the cut. On the twentieth of every month, an armored truck came down Route 147 from Indianapolis. It stopped at seven towns on the way, with Cedar Corners the fourth stop. At each of the towns it dropped off a load of money at the bank, so that each bank would have a good supply of cash the first of the month when a load of people came around with checks to be cashed. The truck, according to Burl, carried between fifty and a hundred thousand dollars each trip. The money was in small bills for the most part, some fifties but the bulk in fives and tens and twenties.

The biggest truckload of the season would come August 20th. That was when most of the farmers in the area had heavy checks for their crops. Hit the armored car then and the take should be at least a hundred thou, maybe more.

McLeod sucked on his cigarette. If they did it, they would need four or five men. They'd hit the truck up around Centreville, just before it stopped to unload money at the Centreville Bank. Centreville was the second stop. If they tried to hit the truck before the first stop at Paulling, they'd be too close to Indianapolis. They'd lose a few bucks this way, but it would be safer.

"More coffee, Marty."

It was the bald man. McLeod filled a fresh cup for him and gave it to him. He went back, finished his cigarette.

Burl made it sound awfully easy. They would stop the truck, show some guns, empty it into a truck of their own, and drive away. That was all there was to it. But if you thought it over it didn't seem that easy. The truck would be carrying guards, and the guards would be carrying guns. There would be shooting. Somebody might get killed. And if they left the guards alive there would be men who could identify them, and they'd spend a long time running. So it probably meant murder—a fast hit, with a batch of corpses left to rot on an Indiana road.

For murder—first-degree murder, murder occurring in the commission of a felony—they did not wink at you and give you a quickie sentence at McAllister. For murder they threw everything at you, and they put you in Death Row, and they strapped you into a chair and threw a switch and let you ride the lightning.

That's what they called it—riding the lightning. And that's what you got when a robbery led to homicide. The state killed you in turn and called it even.

He started another cigarette, drank some coffee. It was hard to think straight now. He hadn't even been thinking of committing a crime until Burl talked to him. He'd been cooling his heels in Cedar Corners, waiting for something and not knowing what the something was, and Burl had sprung the whole deal for him and given him a chance to get in. It meant twenty grand for him if he wanted it. Twenty grand give or take a couple of bucks.

Which wasn't bad.

Yet he didn't really need the money. He had as much dough as he needed, more than he needed. He spent each week's paycheck in the course of the following week simply because he saw no reason to save money, but he still had a few hundred dollars in the bank, and he'd probably have it forever.

So he didn't need the money. He could stay in Cedar Corners, and he could keep on screwing Joyce Ramsdell or somebody like her whenever he felt like it, and he could keep on slinging hash at the Land's End Grill and drinking bourbon at the Corners Tavern. It was easy enough, really.

Why was he interested, then?

Excitement, maybe. Excitement, a desire to get swinging with life again, a hunger for more than he had.

Something like that.

Because he had been alive once, before a certain wife of his had opened her thighs for a certain victim of his, and it had been nice to be alive. He wasn't alive now. He was existing without living, and that was no good. From the moment he caught his wife with the man, he had not been wholly alive.

If he threw in with Burl, he would be a criminal. Not just for the time being, but forever. They'd pushed him in that direction when they sent him to the pen; anybody who went into McAllister came out a criminal for life. They'd given him a push and if he went along with Burl then the die would be cast. It was up to him. He could play it straight or crooked. Either way, this would determine the pattern for the rest of his life.

The money didn't really matter, not when you came right down to it. Hell, it would be nice enough to have twenty grand. It would be great. There were always things you could do with that kind of money, places you could go, women you could coax into the rack. You could live big when you had real money to throw around. And when the money was gone there would always be another job to pull, another robbery to carry off, another way to get your hands on the big dough and take a heavy payoff in return for a heavy risk.

But it wasn't the money. If he had cared much about money he would have gone somewhere other than Cedar Corners and he would have gotten a more lucrative position than counterman at the Land's End Cafe. The money was nice, you couldn't turn up your nose at it, but there was something else. Call it excitement, call it being alive again, call it anything. He'd been sitting around waiting, and it looked as though this was what he had been waiting for all along.

And if everything went sour? It could be bad then. Back to McAllister, only this time instead of a one-year softie they would give him a five-to-ten or a ten-to-twenty, with no clear chance for parole. And if a guard caught a slug somewhere along the way it would be the big one and they would fry for it. The last thing you felt in this world would be the electricity jolting through your body and taking you out for the count.

All these names for it. Riding the lightning. The hot squat.

Crazy to run that kind of risk, just for money, just for excitement.

Other hand, look at the risks he took without thinking about them. Every time he took a drink, every time he smoked a cigarette. Nobody said booze and tobacco were good for you. But he couldn't imagine life without them.

Well, he didn't have to say right away. He'd told Burl he wanted twenty-four hours to think it over, and that was cool with Burl. The job was almost a month off, if they pulled it, and Burl wasn't in that much of a rush. Even with the time it would take to plan it, they didn't have to hurry.

Twenty-four hours. He had about fourteen left to make up his mind one way or the other.

It would be plenty of time.

Virginity is a lousy drag.

Those five words, with a total of twenty-one letters, appeared on a sheet of paper in front of Betty Marie James. She looked at them for a moment, then realized that, by God, she had actually written them without knowing it. She looked at the sheet of paper, then at the pencil which she was still holding in her right hand. She put down the pencil and tore the sheet of paper in half, in half again, in half a third time, in half a fourth time. She wound up with sixteen bits of paper, and she carried them to the wastebasket and threw them away. If anybody happened to go through her wastebasket, put them together like a jigsaw puzzle, and read the result, he would know that she wasn't too keen on virginity. But she didn't think anyone was too likely to do that.

Not too keen on virginity. Now *there* was a thought. It wasn't as simple as that. It wasn't that she was not *keen* on virginity, for God's sake.

She hated it.

She was in her bedroom and the house was empty. She got up, went downstairs and out of the house. It was a Saturday, a particularly hot July Saturday, and she didn't have a thing to do. She was still a little shaky inside after the night with Luke, and she was still depressed. She walked along the street. The sky was cloudless, a deep and abiding blue from horizon to horizon. She felt the heat of the sun on her bare arms. A hot day. A scorcher.

She was dressed for it. She was wearing a sleeveless yellow cotton blouse and a pair of clam-diggers, bright red pants that extended halfway from knee to ankle. She walked along with her hands in her pockets, keeping her elbows back so that her breasts jutted against the front of the blouse. She kicked at a discarded paper cup and the soles of her scuffed loafers raised dust from the sidewalk.

There were two drugstores on Main Street, one called Loewe's Pharmacy and the other called Jim and Ray's Drugs.

People took their prescriptions to Loewe's Pharmacy and bought their condoms at Jim and Ray's Drugs. Loewe's had a soda fountain. She went inside, filled her lungs with conditioned air, and ordered a chocolate malted with an egg in it. The boy who made it for her was named Lester. He was nineteen years old, he had bad acne, and there was a rumor floating around to the effect that he had gotten a girl in trouble in Paulling, but no one was sure. If he had gotten a girl in trouble, Betty Marie thought, the girl must have been blind. Lester was as ugly as a sway-backed hog with warts.

Lester made the malted, set it down in front of her, and leaned forward so that he could get a quick peek at the tops of her breasts. *Cheap thrill for the day,* Betty Marie thought. *Now you can go in the back room, you moron, and you can think about my tits while you play with yourself.*

She was halfway through with the malted when Jimmy Kell walked in. He came over to her, hopped up onto the stool next to her.

"Your man was looking for you," he said.

"Who?"

"Luke," he said. "Who else?"

Anybody else, she thought. Anyone who's a man instead of a silly boy.

"He was wandering around," Jimmy said. "Said he was looking for you and couldn't find you. If you want to get a hold of him, you could try—"

"I don't," she said.

He looked at her. He was a big kid, young and

raw-boned, with muscles in his arms and brightness in his eyes. "Whoa," he said. "You got a lot of feeling into two little words. Something happen with you kids?"

She wanted to laugh. "Nothing happened," she said. Nothing happened—and that was the whole trouble.

"You got a mad on for Luke?"

She didn't answer.

"Luke," he said, "is a pretty nice guy."

"He's a nice boy," she said.

"Oh," he said. "I think I get it."

"Do you?"

"Sure. He's a nice boy and you want a nice man."

"I want a man," she said. "He doesn't have to be nice."

She heard the words, then realized that she had said them. It was too late to call them back now. She saw the knowing look in Jimmy Kell's eyes, the slight smile that was spreading on his thin lips, grinned at her.

"Uh-huh," he said. "I get it."

She didn't say anything.

"Tonight," he said. "Seven-thirty. I'll pick you up and show you what a man's like."

She still didn't say anything.

"Luke's a nice boy," he went on. "Serious, sensible. He's gonna settle down, run that service station of his old man's and go on pumping gas until he drops dead. I'll pick you up half past seven, Betty Marie. We'll have a good time."

*   *   *

When Joyce woke up she had the shakes. She started to wake up around eight in the morning, hungover to beat the band, but she took a gulp of air and pulled the covers over her head and fell back asleep. That held her for the next five hours. Then she opened her eyes again and it was one in the afternoon, and there was nothing to do but get out of bed.

She got out of bed. Then she had to sit down in a hurry because her knees were ready to give out and her head was reeling. She sat down heavily. She had felt worse in her life—once after a night of pub-crawling in Chicago that left her coming to in an alley with stains all over the front of her dress and very little memory of the preceding evening, another time with the circumstances much the same except that the stains were made of blood. But now she was waking up in her own goddamned house and she felt like hell.

She stank, too, and she could smell herself. She had sweated like a pig in her sleep, and it had been hot and she'd slept under all the blankets, and as a result she was coated with her own sweat. And her mouth tasted as though some goat had crapped in it, and her muscles were sore all through, and she wished quite seriously that she could quietly and painlessly die.

McLeod.

She remembered now—his mood, his sexless attitude, his abrupt and unfortunate departure. Then the bottle, and now she was alone and hungover and God it was terrible.

She didn't trust the shower. It would be too easy to slip the way her legs felt. She filled the tub with hot water and got into it and soaked. The bath took some of the ache out of her body and all of the filth from her skin, and when she felt halfway human again she got out of the tub and made instant coffee. She didn't want to wait for water to boil, and not for the first time she used hot tap water. That was a way to make instant coffee even worse than it was under the best of circumstances, but she didn't care, and she drank three cups of it black with sugar. That helped, and food would have helped even more, but she had a feeling that she would only puke it up if she managed to get it down in the first place.

On the radio, a hillbilly was singing country blues—

> *I'm lonesome as a hound-dog, bayin' at a yaller moon;*
> *I'm lonesome as a hound-dog, bayin' at a yaller moon;*
> *Gonna bark and howl if you don't love me soon—*

Oh, Jesus, she thought. Oh God. It would be hard enough to stomach on a perfectly ordinary morning, but when you were hungover it was impossible.

> *I'm crazy as a catfish, swimmin' in a muddy pool;*
> *I'm crazy as a catfish, swimmin' in a muddy pool;*
> *When you run off I felt like an awful fool—*

There was a limit. She turned off the radio, took a slice of bread, bit off a hunk of it, chewed it for a minute, then spat it into the garbage pail unswallowed. Food was just out of the question. She could only sit, and wait, and after awhile the hangover might go away.

It was just about gone by four. She felt better then but she didn't still couldn't face the idea of cooking. She walked over to the Land's End, a cigarette in her mouth, and she ordered a plate of eggs and sausages. The counterman leered at her—what the hell, everybody in Cedar Corners leered at her, it was part of the game when you were the only card-carrying tramp in town. She leered back, and then she wolfed down the eggs and sausages and left.

Hotter than hell outside. She walked home smoking another cigarette, threw it in the gutter and went into the house. The phone was ringing. She answered it and it was McLeod.

"Hello," she said. "How they hanging?"

That would usually get a laugh, but not today. "Listen," he said. "About tonight."

"When are you coming?"

"I'm not."

"Huh?"

"I got something on," he said.

"All night?"

"Just about."

"Then come over now, Marty."

"No."

She hesitated. "Listen," she said, "something's the matter. What is it?"

"Nothing's the matter."

"Then—"

"I got something on the fire," he said.

"Something on the fire. You got some broad on the fire, you bastard."

"No."

"Some hot-pants broad. I'm not enough for you, McLeod? I don't give you enough of a charge."

"I know this is hard to believe," he said, "but this is not about you."

"Then what's the trouble?"

"I got something cooking. I told you, Joyce."

"Listen—"

"You listen," he said. "You don't own me, baby. You want to ball somebody else, go ahead. We've got no strings on each other, so that means you've got nothing to pull. Remember?"

She didn't say anything.

"I got a guy to see," he said. "It's business. I'll see you around."

He hung up on her.

She stood for a moment, holding onto the receiver, glaring at it. Then, swiftly, she slammed it down and marched across the room. She threw her hefty body down into a chair, reached for a fresh cigarette, lit it. She smoked it in a hurry and stabbed it out in the ash tray.

The bastard, she thought. The rotten bastard.

He was taking her for granted. In a way, that wasn't especially surprising. Men had taken Joyce Ramsdell for granted for a long time, largely because she was the type of broad who was generally taken for granted. Sweetheart of the Navy, everyman's girl, that type of scene.

But McLeod had been different. With McLeod, she had been content to make it with one man and only one man. And now McLeod was tossing her over for some pig, dropping her by the side of the road the way a horse dropped a load.

Well, screw McLeod!

You want to ball somebody else, just go ahead. That was what the bastard had said. Well, why not take the bastard at his word. Why not find some other stud and make it with him? McLeod didn't own her any more than she owned McLeod. So why not?

She changed her clothes, put on a skirt and a sweater. It was too hot to wear a sweater, but she didn't particularly give a damn. In the first place, she didn't figure to be wearing it very long. In the second place, she liked the way she looked in a sweater. Her breasts stuck out a mile and you could see the outlines of the goddamn nipples when she wasn't wearing a bra.

You want to ball somebody else, just go ahead.

Oh, you Marty McLeod, she thought. Oh, you rat bastard son of a bitch. Oh, you goddamn world, why didn't anything ever work out right, why did things always get screwed up?

Why?

There was only one thing to do when everything got screwed up. You could drink, but drinking only numbed it and left you feeling like the bottom of a birdcage when you came down from your high. So the only thing to do was to find a man—or an army—and take that man to bed. Sex was a kind of therapy. Joyce had used it for that purpose all her life. There was no reason to stop now.

Marty McLeod, she thought. No strings, no love words, none of that garbage. But she was in love with him anyway, and the bastard didn't know or didn't care, and that left her hung up as usual and down as usual and, as a direct result, itchy.

As usual.

She went out of the door, into the heat. She walked, head set, shoulders tossed back, big boobs straining at the sweater front. She walked, legs moving like machinery, rear swaying gently, eyes scanning the streets for a man.

Any man.

Any man at all.

She was sitting in the living room when he pulled up in front of the house and leaned on the horn. Her mother glanced up, then turned to her with a puzzled expression on her face.

"Luke got a new car?"

"No," Betty Marie said.

"That doesn't look like Luke's car, dear."

"It's not."

"Then—"

"It's not Luke," she said. "Bye, Ma."

She hurried out the door. Jimmy Kell was sitting behind the wheel of an old Pontiac convertible which he had picked up for fifty dollars, labored over for a few weeks, and finally painted an unfortunate yellow-green. He'd hit that particular color by mixing a couple cans of paint together, and in spots the paint had tended to unmix itself while drying to create a curiously mottled effect, something like a World War II tank camouflaged for jungle warfare in the Solomons.

There were two rumors circulating in reference to the convertible. The first held that the car had hit one-fifteen on Route 147 once, had outrun two state troopers' cars and somehow ducked a roadblock without anyone catching the number. The other referred not to the speed of the car but to the speed of the driver, alleging that the back seat had been dyed red by the blood of virgins whom Jimmy had initiated into the mysteries of love. Jimmy did everything in his power to encourage both of these rumors.

He threw the door open for Betty Marie. She climbed in, and he gunned the motor and popped the clutch, taking off with a squeal and leaving a patch of rubber on the pavement.

"Wild," he said. "You look good tonight, Betty Marie."

She smiled.

"Happy?"

"Sure."

"That's good. You've been going out with Luke for a long time, haven't you?"

"What's that got to do with anything?"

He shrugged easily. "Just a question," he said. "How long do you figure the two of you have been going together?"

"A long time. Close to a year."

"So you must be used to a special kind of date," he went on. "Now I ought to know something about that date so I can show you the kind of time you like. What do you and Luke do when you go out?"

"We just go out."

"Well—"

"We go for a ride," she said. "Or we go to a movie, like we did last night. Or we go to the Land's End for a soda."

"Sounds exciting."

She ignored the sarcasm. "Sometimes we drive out of town and see a picture at a drive-in," she said.

"Do you neck?"

"Uh-huh."

"Do you have to go to a drive-in for that?"

"Guess not."

"Well," he said. "What do you figure you want to do tonight, Betty Marie?"

"Whatever you want."

They were past the town line now. The convertible top was down and the air rustled her hair, tossing it back and forth. She liked the way it played with her yellow hair, liked the feel of it. She felt all free and loose and happy.

"Open the glove compartment, Betty Marie."

It was unlocked. She opened it and took out a brown paper bag. There was a bottle in it. She drew out the bottle. It was a brown glass bottle with no label on it. Because of the color of the glass she could not determine the color of the liquor inside.

"Shine," he said. "Good Kentucky corn, best money can buy. You ever have shine, Betty Marie?"

"No."

"I don't guess we'll need a drive-in movie," he said. "I guess we'll just tug this buggy off the road, and we'll take the cap off that pint of shine, and we'll do ourselves some social drinking. Ever get high as the moon, girl?"

She shook her head. A few beers once, enough to make her dizzy, enough to make her sleepy. Nothing more than that. The shine would be something else again. She moved closer to him, put her head on his broad shoulder. He reached around her with one arm and cupped her shoulder with his large hand. He drove the car with the other hand and did not let up on the accelerator.

You don't have to get me drunk, she wanted to say. *I'll let you fuck me, I want you to fuck me, and you don't have to get me drunk first.*

She didn't say anything.

"Open the bottle," he said. "Have a drink."

She uncapped the brown bottle and put it to her lips, taking a tentative sip of the liquid. It was very strong. She swallowed a mouthful and it burned its way down into her stomach. She coughed; coughed again. He took the bottle from her and took a long swallow from it.

"You shouldn't drink while you drive," she said.

He laughed. "Maybe you shouldn't," he said. "You ain't too used to shine. Now me, I been drinking shine since I was thirteen. Believe that? I'm not like your boy Luke,

Betty Marie. I don't figure to play jockey to a gas pump for the rest of my life."

She looked at him. "What are you going to do?"

"This and that." He shrugged loosely. "You know a fellow named Charlie Ives?"

She didn't.

"They call him Burl," he said. "On account of he's fat, like Burl Ives. Nobody ever calls him anything but Burl, but his name's Charles Ives, We're friends, Burl and me."

"So?"

"So nothing. So a guy can do all right being a friend of Burl's. I ain't worrying any, Betty Marie."

And then he was cutting off on a side road, pressing the accelerator down to the floor. The tires scattered pebbles in front of them. He drove for half a mile, then pulled off the road and cut the engine. He took another long drink from the bottle of shine and passed it to her. She tilted it, took a longer swallow this time. At first she felt nothing; then the burning sensation brought tears to her eyes and she began coughing spasmodically.

"Hey," he said. "Easy. Just sort of take it a sip at a time, Betty Marie. That way it don't get to you all at once. Now try it again, just a little sip."

She took a smaller swallow this time. It still burned, but it was better this time, a pleasant sensation instead of a distinctly unpleasant one. She tried to decide whether she was drunk or not. She felt the same as always. If it was having any effect on her, she hadn't noticed it yet.

"More," he said.

She took another sip, then another. She gave the bottle to him and watched him drain it, leaving only a little shine in the very bottom. "Might as well kill it," he said, giving her the bottle. "No sense bringing home a swallow. Finish her off."

She finished it off. He took the bottle from her hand and tossed it over the side of the car. It must have hit a rock when it landed, because she heard the bottle shatter to bits. He turned to face her again and she closed her eyes and waited for him to kiss her.

He kissed her.

His mouth had a good cigarette-and-moonshine taste. She surrendered herself completely to the kiss, letting his tongue shoot deep into her mouth, pressing his body and hers close together, feeling his chest against her breasts. Only then did she realize how much effect the shine was having on her. Her head was lighter than air, floating free and easy. She kissed him hard, felt the beginnings of deep passion rising in her body.

He said: "I got another pint of shine in the trunk."

"Get it."

"There's a blanket there, too."

"Get them both."

She waited, head tossed back on the seat and eyes closed, while he got out of the car and walked around to the back. He came back with a blanket and the second pint of shine.

She let him help her out of the car. They walked in deep grass, and he spread out the blanket and sat down on it, pulling her down beside him. He kissed her, and this time she used her tongue to excite him. It worked. He pulled her down on the blanket, kissing her expertly. She moved her legs around him, starting to sway with her hips. They were both still fully clothed but the motions were exciting anyway and she felt her head swimming and her heart pounding.

He rolled off her, uncapped the shine. He took a drink. She opened her mouth, and he held the bottle to her lips while she gulped the strong corn whiskey. He took the bottle away from her, capped it, and began to unbutton her blouse. She lay still while he took it off. When he removed her bra, his fingers were not clumsy as Luke's always were. He was deft and skillful. She wondered how many bras he had removed from various girls in his time. Probably hundreds of them.

"The greatest tits in Cedar Corners," he said.

"You like them?"

"Make that the whole state of Indiana," he said. He took one in each hand and squeezed. He buried his face between them, rubbing his cheeks against the sides of her breasts. She was on fire now, flaming, aching inside.

She took the bottle from him. She had another drink, then grinned wickedly at him.

"You want a drink?"

"Sure," he said.

Still grinning, she poured shine on both her breasts, then spilled some more in the valley between them.

"Drink," she said.

He drank. He kissed the liquid from her breasts, kissed

the moonshine from each large mound in turn, and he turned her into a dynamo of passion. She felt as though her breasts were on fire, burning with passion. She didn't wait for him to take off her skirt and panties, but did this herself, ripping off her clothing until she was naked. Then she squirmed involuntarily on the blanket, writhing like a segmented worm.

"Do it," she moaned. "Make love to me!"

He stripped himself naked. He touched her, handled her, played with the animalistic heat of her being. And then his fingers were gone and there was something else there, something nicer than any finger on earth.

He touched her, poked at her. And then he tore her in half and made her shriek like a banshee into the summer night. The pain was tremendous, inconceivable, a huge shooting pain that spread to every corner of her being.

Pain.

Awful, awful pain.

And then, with his body moving within her, moving irresistibly and eternally within her, the pain began to disappear. It waned, paled and then it was gone and there was a wave of sweetness in its place.

The sweetness didn't go away.

Instead, it got sweeter.

And sweeter.

Until she was matching his movements with movements of her own, churning her body and then the world began to take off, began to swing and thrust and vibrate, and the roof flew off and the sky fell in and came apart at the seams.

Until she got there, way out free and clear and on top of the world, and it was sweetness and light and an explosion and a tidal wave and everything, all at once, and then peace.

She wanted to lie still forever. But, after a moment, he was sitting up.

"Was I good?"

"You're a mountain lion," he said. "A cross between a rabbit and a mountain lion. You're fire, Betty Marie."

She didn't say anything.

"First time," he said. "Wasn't it?"

She nodded.

"Poor old Luke," he said. "That gas pumper doesn't know a good thing when you shove it under his nose."

She sighed, leaned back on the blanket. She felt divine, like a queen or a goddess. She felt wonderful. The air was cool on her bare skin and her head was still spinning happily from the moonshine and she felt wonderful.

If this was what the first time was like, she could just imagine how fine it would be when she actually knew what she was doing.

Chapter 4

He hardly knew what was happening. First the date with Betty Marie, and then dropping her off and driving crazily to Rushville, and picking up the whore in the bar and taking her to her room and learning, suddenly, what sex was all about. Then the trip back, and sleeping most of the day, and then, after dinner, driving over to pick up Betty Marie.

Who hadn't been home.

"She went out, Luke," her mother told him. "Some boy came round for her and she went out with him. He had a convertible, you know, with the top down. I don't know who it was."

Luke had known. It must have been Jimmy Kell, and if Betty was out with Jimmy Kell she'd better watch herself. He remembered what he and the Rushville whore had done, and he thought of Betty Marie doing the same sort of thing with Jimmy Kell, and he thought he was going to puke. He got mad, fighting mad, but by the time he was downtown again the mad had worn off and he barely felt a thing. All he knew was that everything was happening in one hell of a hurry and he couldn't keep up with it. A day ago everything had been all clear-cut and simple. Then Betty Marie had surprised him by wanting him to do it to her, and then he had gone and done it for ten dollars with a whore in Rushville, and now Betty Marie was off with Jimmy Kell and God alone knew what was happening.

A day ago, he knew where he stood. He'd graduate, marry Betty Marie, have kids, and live happily ever after.

Now he wasn't so certain. Maybe his mother was right, maybe a boy should kick up his heels and have a time for himself before he thought about settling down. Of course, he loved Betty Marie. Well, didn't he?

God, he wasn't sure about a thing any more. Maybe he didn't love her at all. Maybe what he got from the whore was all he'd ever really wanted from Betty Marie, and he'd wanted it so much he mistook it for love. Maybe he'd been fool enough to tell himself he wanted the whole package, the wife and kids and mortgaged house, when all he wanted was sex.

He stopped to hand roll a cigarette. It came out okay, good enough to smoke. He lit it, then leaned against a building. He saw the woman coming, breasts swaying and mouth all pouty, and while ordinarily he would not have said hello to her, this was something of a special occasion.

He called: "Hi there, Joyce!"

By rights he should have called her Mrs. Ramsdell. After all, she was almost thirty and she had been married once. But she wasn't the kind of woman you called Mrs. Ramsdell. She was a tramp, and you had to call tramps by their first names.

"Hi," she said.

Ten minutes later they were back at her house having coffee together. Five minutes after that she had her sweater off, and she was leaning back in her chair and letting him play with her huge breasts. He took them in his mouth and sucked the nipples and got so excited he was ready to scream.

Five minutes later they were on the bed, and a few minutes after that he was inside her, and Jesus but it felt good. Better than with the whore in Rushville, and he didn't see how it could feel any better with Betty Marie.

McLeod stalled Burl. He met him at Big John's at six, and he told him he hadn't decided yet.

"Jesus," Burl said. "You're in or you're out, Marty. Let's get cracking."

"I got to think," McLeod said.

"What's to think?"

"I have to make up my mind."

"When do you know?"

"Tonight," McLeod promised. "Tonight, one way or the other. That's a promise. It's definite."

Burl nodded. McLeod left Big John's and walked over Limestone to Main, then headed uptown on Main Street. He scratched a match, lit a cigarette, inhaled, blew out smoke.

At the Corners Tavern he stopped for a quick double,

tossed it off and paid for it. Then he headed uptown again. He wasn't sure where the hell he was going. Burl wanted him in on the deal, and in a way he wanted to be in, but at the same time he felt dubious about it. What the hell—when you came right down to it, he had a good thing going as it stood. He had a job that was easy and steady, a broad who was just as easy and just as steady. He had everything he wanted but excitement, and he wasn't sure he wanted that.

Stick around, he thought. Cool it, relax, keep on slinging hash and banging Joyce and belting the bottle. Maybe, God knows, you might wake up some day and straighten out. Go to another state and start being a lawyer again.

It could happen.

He lit a fresh cigarette, realized he was walking toward Joyce's house. Well, why not? He'd been pretty rough with her on the phone, snapping at her like that, and she didn't deserve it. He wasn't too crazy for the idea of taking her to bed but it would be something to do, and once he was in bed with her he'd forget how disinterested he was. She had that effect on a man, bless her. She was the wildest thing in the world, and she could go all night without tiring, and they made a good pair.

Something kept him from ringing her doorbell. Something made him look in the window first. The living room was empty of people, but there was clothing all over. Joyce's clothing. And a man's clothing.

He walked up the driveway and behind the house. He went over to the bedroom window, looked in.

And stared.

Joyce was on the bed, and she was naked, and she had company. The kid with her couldn't have been more than sixteen or seventeen and he didn't look as though he knew too much about what he was doing. But he didn't really have to, McLeod thought. She sure as hell did. She knew enough for both of them.

He watched the kid handling her breasts, watched her grab him and fondle him. She rolled over onto her back then, pulling him aboard, and the kid did what he was supposed to do, and McLeod turned away and took three steps before he threw up. He almost hit his shoes. He let his stomach turn itself inside-out, heaved and heaved, and when he was done he felt better.

A tramp, he thought.

Just a tramp. All right, he had told her to ball someone else if she needed it that badly. All right, they had a thing going with no strings attached. It didn't make a bit of difference. She was his broad as long as they lasted, and she was his private piece, and if she was passing it around she could drop dead as far as he was concerned.

Women.

They weren't worth a damn, he thought. There wasn't a woman in the world who wouldn't fuck like a rabbit if you gave her the chance. They were all alike, and you could take every last one of them and cram them down a toilet somewhere.

Women.

At least this time all he'd done was vomit. Last time he'd

seen something like this, he'd reached for a knife. And what
had that bought him?

He lit a fresh cigarette, laughed bitterly. He was walking quickly now, his palms damp with sweat, his eyes fierce.
He laughed again. Stick around, he told himself scornful-
ly. Keep your job and your woman and tell yourself what a
sweet and swinging place Cedar Corners can be. Shove it,
mister. Take it and cram it and leave me out of it, please.

He came to the Corners Tavern and started through the
door, then stopped very suddenly. No, he thought. No, the
drinking was another part of it that you could write off as
a bad deal all around. Drinking was for losers, and it had
been fine for him for a long time, and it wasn't fine any longer. There was a point where drinking was necessary. When
you were on the bottom, and when you were not trying to
get back on top again, drinking made a certain degree of
sense.

But when you were ready to come back to life, the first
thing you had to do was dry yourself out. You didn't need
the bottle then. You generated your own kind of excitement, swung with it and for it, and a couple of shots would
only tend to cramp your style.

He left the tavern and continued on down Main to Limestone. He passed the Land's End Cafe and looked across the
street at it. Waste yourself slinging hash at a cheap bean-
ery and boozery—what kind of a life was that for a human
being? Fine, if you didn't have any brains. Double-fine, if
you didn't have any guts. No good at all if you had brains
and guts together. Then it was a waste of time and energy,

and you only had so much of each in your lifetime, and you were a damned fool to waste them.

On Limestone, he went into Big John's and looked for Burl. The fat man wasn't there. He went to the counter, had a cup of coffee and asked the huge Greek where Burl was. The Greek told him to try the malt shop a few doors down. McLeod went there, and Burl was there spooning ice cream into his fat face.

"Well?" Burl said.

"In," McLeod said. "In all the way."

"You sure?"

"Never surer."

Burl stuck out a hand and McLeod shook it. The fat man was happy—it showed in his eyes and his smile. He clapped a hand on McLeod's shoulder and squeezed.

"What decided you, Marty?"

"Things."

"What?"

"The hell," McLeod said. "Burl, you wouldn't believe me if I told you."

It was Sunday.

On Sunday morning, Cedar Corners went to church. The single Jewish doctor didn't, of course, but he was an exception to the rule and an understandable one. Outside of him, anyone who didn't go to church on Sunday in Cedar

Corners was a rotten atheist, and probably a Commie to boot.

Jimmy Kell didn't go to church. He wasn't alone in this respect, but he was one of the few high school kids who didn't make excuses for not attending church. In his words, it was a load of crap and he didn't need it.

This Sunday he was driving from Cedar Corners to Centreville. He left Cedar Corners at precisely nine in the morning. He put the Pontiac's accelerator fairly close to the floor, and he aimed the car north and east on 147, and he drove. In the course of the past week he had performed some important repairs on the car, had tuned the engine perfectly, had replaced the plugs and tightened the shocks and souped things up a bit. The Pontiac convertible was now in perfect shape.

Jimmy drove well. There were certain things which interested him, and he did these things very well. Other less interesting things he did not bother with at all. Cars interested him; as a result, he could take one apart and put it together again as well as the best mechanic in Rushville, and he could drive the wheels off it once it was in shape. Girls interested him, and he rode them as intensely as he rode the Pontiac, racing their engines, downshifting on the curves, and popping the clutch now and then just to make them jump.

Money interested him, too. Not the slow money, the kind you worked your ass off for and spent before you had it. That was sucker money and the suckers were welcome to it.

His kind was fast money. That was the only kind there was, really, as far as one James Kell was concerned. The kind you got in a hurry, easy as pie, and it was all yours when you were done and the only hard work was figuring out how to spend it.

So far it hadn't come that easy. There were little jobs he did for Burl and the barber and a few others, errands and like that, but nothing you could say really paid off. A ten-spot here, a twenty there, and a hell of a lot better than weeding gardens and mowing lawns. But nothing big.

There was big stuff coming.

He concentrated on his driving, pushing the car hard. It took him an hour and thirty-three minutes to hit the city limits of Centreville. He checked his watch, nodded, and turned the car around. He'd figured it an hour and a half, and it had taken just three minutes more than that.

On the way back, he held the car to precisely five miles an hour over the speed limit. He clocked the best time possible at that speed, not losing seconds on turns and not getting stuck behind trucks. On the way back, he thought about Betty Marie.

Now *there* was a broad. When you liked girls, liked what they had under their dresses, you got into plenty of pussies that just weren't worth the trouble. You took what you found, and some were good and some were bad, and the bad ones you never saw again and the good ones gave you a real run for your money.

Betty Marie was one of the good ones.

Hell, that didn't do her justice. One of the good ones? She was a lot more than that.

She was one of the great ones.

A tiger, a goddamn tiger. You didn't expect a virgin to show you much the first time down, any more than you expected to get top performance out of a car the first time you put it through its paces. So Betty Marie had been one hell of a surprise to him. She wasn't afraid and she wasn't ashamed and she wasn't embarrassed and she wasn't clumsy.

She was wild.

And she was going to be a lot of fun, a goddamn ball. He was going to get a lot of Betty Marie in the next month. He was going to show her every trick in the book and a few that nobody had written about yet.

He was going to make her a woman all the way and have all the fun in the world with her.

He grinned, remembering the first time. Not long ago, really. A year and a half, maybe a little closer to two years. He'd been a sharp little bastard even then, older than his years, ready to mix it up with anybody, ready to pick up the fast money wherever it was. Burl had been using him for deliveries at the time. Burl had a thing going, buying up shine and selling it, and Jimmy was delivering for him. He was an ace with a car even then and he would load up the truck with pints and quarts of shine and make the deliveries for Burl.

It was at night, a middle-of-the-week night in late autumn. He smiled, remembering—

*   *   *

The delivery was in Hillcrest, about twenty miles due west of Cedar Corners. Jimmy had two more to make after it. He pushed his car to Hillcrest, found the right house, parked in front and went to the door. There was a bell. He rang it, leaning on it until he heard someone coming. When you were delivering shine you didn't have to have good manners. The customer was always wrong, and usually stoned, so the hell with it.

A broad opened the door.

Not just a broad. A rather special broad, with black hair and blue eyes and a body that was too much to think about. A broad in a housecoat that was sheer enough to let most of that body show. He handed her two quarts of shine and she made no move to take them from him. She just stood there, looking at him.

"From Burl," he said. "You ordered these, didn't you?"

The broad smiled. She was about twenty-three and she was beautiful. She turned from him.

"Sally," she called, "get out here, will you?"

Sally was even better looking. Not as busty, maybe, but beautiful. Soft brown hair, a quiet face, a slim body. Her housecoat was about the same as the brunette's. Jimmy started to sweat. Something was up and he didn't know what.

"Come on in," Sally said. "I'm Sally. This is Eva, my sister. I don't think we know your name—"

"It's Jimmy."

"Hello, Jimmy. Will you have a drink with us?"

"I'm not much on drinking," he said.

"So you'll learn."

He edged toward the door. "I've got more deliveries to make," he said nervously. "Maybe when I got done—"

That was all he said, because Eva grabbed him. She held him in her arms and pressed her body against his. He went tense all over, and then she kissed him, working on him with her mouth. He returned the kiss and rubbed her back through the housedress. He didn't have to think about it. His hands moved by themselves.

The two of them took him to a room with a huge double bed in it. He was still nervous, even more nervous when Eva began to undress him. She took off all his clothes and pushed him on the bed with Sally. He cowered there, scared to look at her nakedness.

"Go on," Sally said. "Don't be afraid."

Then there was nothing to be afraid of. She copped his cherry easily and neatly, and he was still marveling over what had happened when Eva joined them on the bed, grabbing at him. And then it was Eva's turn, and he was making love to her, stabbing blindly into the sweet warm softness of her, proving his manhood a second time only moments after the first time.

They kept him there all night long. They passed him back and forth until he was too tired to move, and then they let him sit there and watch while they did something he had never even heard of before.

"We're sisters," Eva told him.

"We take good care of each other," Sally said.

"Sometimes there aren't any men around—"

"So we do things like this."

And they showed him what they meant. They kissed each other's breasts, and they fondled each other, and their lips did unbelievable things to each other, and he was so excited that he went out of his mind, falling onto the bed, grabbing first one and then the other, possessing and using and slipping away finally, limp and exhausted.

In the morning he went in to take a shower. First Eva joined him under the spray, and then Sally included herself in the party, and they were all there. Sally was behind him, holding him, pressing her small breasts into his back and rubbing her body against his buttocks. Eva was crouching before him, soaping him up, then washing her mouth out with soap in a new and improved fashion that drained him anew. He left, finally, drove back to Cedar Corners, and slept for sixteen hours . . .

He smiled now at the memory. He kept driving. It took him two hours and forty minutes to get back to Cedar Corners at the legal speed plus five miles per hour. He parked the car in front of Big John's and went inside. Burl was there.

"One-thirty-three going," he said. "Two-forty coming back."

Burl nodded.

He went out again. Eva and Sally—what a goddamn pair those two had been! And Betty Marie would be just as good once she learned the ropes. He had a month to get tight with her and he was going to get as tight as possible.

A month.

And, in a month, the world would really start to swing.

In a month he would make himself five thousand dollars. Burl was letting him drive the car—he knew there wasn't a better wheelman in the state. And, after they hit the armored truck, he'd have five thousand bucks for his troubles.

He grinned.

No Longer A Virgin.

That had been the title of a book that Betty Marie read once, a book about a girl who was no longer a virgin from the third chapter onward. An exciting book, as Betty Marie remembered. But the best thing about the book, now that she thought about it, was that the title now described her. She was no longer a virgin, and thank God for that.

Virginity had been a bore. Virginity, and the sort of life that went with it, would leave her married at sixteen or seventeen to Luke Penner and stuck in Cedar Corners for the rest of her life. If that was living, you could take it and keep it. She wasn't interested.

Saturday night, Jimmy Kell had made a woman of her. He'd gotten her smashed on shine, and then he had taught her what it was all about, and it was heaven.

Sunday, she stayed close to home. But that night Jimmy came calling for her and took her for a ride, and they messed up the blanket again, and it was heaven all over again.

And it had gone on in that vein for the past week. Not every night, of course. Jimmy had something on his mind, something that was taking up a lot of his time, and he couldn't be with her as much as she would have liked. But the times he was with her more than made up for the times she was alone. Each time he thrilled her in a new way, and each time was better than the last time, and she thought she was going to go crazy from so much concentrated loving.

It was wonderful.

It was Thursday now, and she was alone. Her mother was out somewhere and her father was working. She sat in the tub, soaking, washing, then got out finally and dried herself off. It was another hot day—every day seemed hotter than the one before it lately. She had nothing to do.

She went into the living room and took a cigarette from the little dish her mother kept on the coffee table. It had a filter on it, and Jimmy had taught her that filtered cigarettes belonged in a class that included watered whiskey and watered-down sex. She snapped off the filter, flipped it into a wastebasket, and lit the cigarette. Without the filter it was extremely strong. She sucked the smoke down into her lungs, held it there for a moment, then exhaled.

She wondered, suddenly, just what had happened to Luke. He hadn't come around since that night, the night before Jimmy made a woman out of her. He had simply disappeared. Once he came for her, and her mother told him she was out. And that was all. It seemed like a pretty funny switch for a guy who had been hungry as hell to marry her.

She ducked ashes from her cigarette, took another long drag. Maybe he had heard the word, she thought. Maybe Jimmy had gotten to him, had told him that he was sleeping with one Betty Marie James and that Luke should stay the hell away. That was one possibility, and it made a certain amount of sense.

Or maybe Luke had simply turned cold. That made a little less sense, but she supposed it was possible. Maybe, just maybe, he was afraid of her. Maybe he'd been thinking of her as something pure and sweet, and maybe that last night had shown him she was a lot hotter than he'd ever realized, and maybe that realization made him turn tail and run like a scared rabbit. Of course, that didn't exactly explain why he turned up Saturday night, while she was with Jimmy. But it seemed fairly sensible.

She ground out the cigarette, leaned back in her chair and sighed. All things considered, she had to admit, Luke Penner was a pretty nice guy. Of course, Jimmy had the word on that. He said nice guys finished last. But Luke was a nice guy, even if he wasn't her type, and she felt sorry for him.

Poor Luke, she thought.

Poor Luke.

"Poor Luke."

Luke was lying on his back, his eyes vaguely focused on the ceiling. He had a hand-rolled cigarette between the middle finger and index finger of his right hand. He brought it to his mouth, dragged on it, let the smoke trickle ceilingward without bothering to inhale.

"You're tired," Joyce was saying. "Aren't you, baby?"

"A little."

"I wear you out, don't I?"

He didn't answer. She learned across him, plucked the cigarette from his hand, pitched it easily out through the open window. He wondered if it would start the yard on fire. Be interesting, he thought. Interesting to watch Joyce running nude down the street and shouting *Fire!* at the top of her lungs. Interesting.

"You worn out, Luke?"

He shook his head. She was hell on wheels, he thought, but she couldn't wear him out. Ever since the day he let her pick him up off the street, he'd been banging her steadily, pounding himself into her night and day. But she didn't wear him out and she never would. Nobody would ever wear him out.

It was funny, he thought. You could go along in a little rut for years, with a certain batch of notions buzzing around in your brain, and you could completely miss the thing you were really cut out for. Here he'd gone on thinking he was designed to marry Betty Marie and have children by her and live a quiet life in a quiet town.

Wrong.

That wasn't his cup of tea at all. Every man has one thing that he does to perfection, one forte in which he really excels. Some men can swim faster than others, and some men can play a better game of tiddlywinks, and some men can keep a hundred different phone numbers in their heads and always remember one right off the bat without making a mistake. Luke had a different strong point, and it was one for which he had been perfectly designed.

He was a sex machine.

Funny, he thought. With Betty Marie, he had been all tied up in knots, all confused and frustrated and afraid to let himself go. With the whore in Rushville it was better and worse all at once. But with Joyce—crazy old Joyce with the willing body and the bountiful bazooms—he could let loose and be himself.

A sex machine.

A stud.

He laughed, a private laugh. Crazy old Joyce was a hungry bitch, he thought. Never got enough. But he was one goddamn stallion who could make her shout uncle. He didn't even like the old girl, hated the way she made a slob of herself, but he couldn't complain about the sex she gave him.

And he liked to beat her at her own game, to come out on top. He liked to slam it into her so much that she couldn't take it any more, so much that she cried and begged and made funny noises and finally, beaten and destroyed, gave up. She always came back for more. He was just a kid, just a punk kid, but she always came back for more, and he always had more ready for her.

"Poor Luke," she was saying.

He didn't move. Now, he thought, was the time to let her squirm. Now was the time to play it extra cool, to lie on his back and watch the ceiling and let her walk up the walls.

That too was fun. It was nice to feel powerful, nice to have a woman beg for it.

"Luke," she said.

She was leaning over him, her legs curled under her ample rear end, her breasts hanging in his face like a pair of ripe melons dripping from the vine. All he had to do was take a little bite of those knockers of hers and she'd scream and jump him. But he didn't do it. He went on playing it cool.

"Luke," she cooed.

Her hand was on his knee. It moved slowly but deliberately up his leg, jumped to his stomach, then moved downward again. It found what it had been looking for and it began to handle with care, fondle with lust, play with passion.

But he still stayed cool. A few more days, he thought. Then you can find yourself another stud, Joycie. You can just hustle up another little boy and show him all you got to offer in the whole wide world.

Because Luke is moving on.

Her hands were both working now. She crouched at his side, moved downward, and her lips were at his throat, kissing and nibbling. He had his hands clasped together behind his neck. He closed his eyes and let her kiss him.

Luke is moving on, he thought. Luke found out what he was put on earth for, and he's going to spread it around. One woman wasn't enough, not by the longest of shots. One woman was enough to get started on, but Cedar Corners was full of women and girls, and he had to try them all. Screw everything you could push over, he told himself.

Give them all a taste, and make them get down on their hands and knees and beg for more.

Now Joyce was kissing his chest. Her tongue snaked out and raced over his smooth skin, and it felt so good that he almost let her know how much he was enjoying it. But he forced himself to be calm. He breathed deeply and steadily while her head moved lower and her lips found new worlds to cherish. Her lips flicked to his navel, stayed there a moment or two, then traveled further south. He let his own lips curl in a mean smile.

A townful of womenfolk, he thought happily. There were married ones and single ones, old ones and young ones. There was a young widow on Walnut Street with the sweetest-looking knobs in the world, and there was a redhead in his class at high school with a butt that wiggled while she walked, and there was—

Oh, there were many of them.

And he would have them all.

Some of them were aching for it. Before he hadn't recognized the signs, but that had been a million moans and groans ago and he was no longer the boy he had been, no longer the frightened kid who would reach for a Band-Aid if he ever saw that sweet and lovely wound that never heals. Now he would know the signs, and he would not pass up a good bet.

Others weren't aching for it. Others were perfectly content the way they were, but that was just too damned bad. He would work on them, and he would play them like catfish on a line, and he would come out a winner. He'd make the virgins come across the line, and he'd make the faithful wives double-cross their trusting husbands, and he'd make the old maids give in and take it and love it. He was going to have himself a goddamn ball.

"Luke."

He lay there, eyes closed. Joyce Ramsdell said his name once more, and then her lips did something lovable, and then her mouth opened and closed and she did not speak his name any more, did not say a thing.

She couldn't.

It was impossible.

The sensations were dizzying, delicious. He let pleasure wash over him, took it passively without moving a muscle. He let her do her wild tricks, and he let her hands fondle him in special places to accentuate the pleasure, and he just stayed there with his eyes closed and let her make him feel like God.

And suddenly, near the end, his mind filled with another image. Joyce was no longer Joyce at all. Joyce was Betty Marie James, and she was kneeling before him with her eyes dripping terror, and she was doing unto him as Joyce was doing unto him now, jaws working and lips quivering and eyes fearful.

The image thrilled him. And he focused on it, concentrated on it, and quivered spasmodically, letting Joyce harvest the sweet fruits of his fulfillment.

Chapter 5

They were in McLeod's shack on the edge of town. McLeod was sitting on a straight-backed wooden chair. He had a cigarette in one hand and a cup of coffee in the other. The coffee was too hot. He was smoking the cigarette and waiting for the coffee to cool.

Burl was lying on the sofa drinking rye whiskey from a paper cup. He sat up slowly, looking at McLeod through beady eyes. He tossed off his drink and poured more rye into the cup.

"You ain't drinking," he said.

"I don't drink much," McLeod told him.

"I heard different."

"That was before," McLeod said. "I wasn't working then. I don't drink when I work."

It was the truth. He hadn't been drinking at all since he made his choice and threw in with Burl. The drinking hadn't been a disease. It had been a time-killer and a pain-killer and that was all. It dulled things, smoothed them out, turned angles into soft curves. But he didn't need it any more. Now the world was alive and he was waiting for something big and exciting, and he didn't need the liquor. He didn't want it. The angles were important now, the soft curves something to be avoided. He hadn't had more than one drink in the course of a day since he joined with Burl, and most days he stuck with coffee all through. It was better for him that way.

Burl said: "Whatever works, that's what you stick with."

"Yeah."

"I drink when I'm working. I have to, Marty. That's when I need it. I get calm then and not nervous."

"Why be nervous? We got two weeks."

"That's not much."

"It's enough. Anyway, how come you drink rye? I would of thought you'd be drinking corn."

"I sell that slop. I don't drink it myself."

McLeod laughed. He sipped his coffee, swallowed. He dragged on his cigarette, dropped the butt on the floor of the shack and ground it out under his heel. He didn't leave it there. A pig like Joyce Ramsdell would have left it there, but McLeod wasn't a pig. He picked up the butt and pitched it into a copper wastebasket.

"I wanted to fill you in," Burl said.

"Shoot."

"I got the people all lined up, Marty. I got two boys from out of town. You don't know them."

"Friends of yours?"

"I worked with them before, Marty. There's a fellow named Jack Dawes and a fellow named Mike Lieber, both of them strong boys with a lot of heart. Not chickens."

"Can they stand the gaff?"

"No sweat, Marty."

"Tell me about 'em."

Burl nodded slowly. "This Jack," he said. "Two stretches, one at McAllister and one at Joliet. The first was for assault with intent and the second was armed robbery. He can handle any kind of gun in the world and he's not afraid to use his fists."

"Go on."

"Mike was never sent up. Also good with a gun, and he happens to own a chopper. We still have to buy another one, but his chopper is good to have. You know what it costs to pick up a tommy gun, Marty?"

He'd heard at McAllister. "Around two grand," he said.

"Close to three. That's Mike. He doesn't talk much, hardly says a word. But he's tough."

McLeod nodded. "That leaves one to go," he said.

"Yeah."

"Who?"

"The driver," Burl said. "The guy who has to push the main car and make time when it counts. I got somebody in town for that."

"Who?"

"Jimmy Kell."

"Do I know him?"

"Maybe. He delivers for me."

McLeod stared. "Oh, Christ," he said. "You have to be nuts, Burl. You have to be crazy."

"Something wrong?"

"He's a kid, dammit!"

Burl drank more rye, crushed the paper cup in his fat hand. "He's the best man behind a wheel I ever saw in my life," he said slowly, easily. "He can do things with a car you wouldn't dream about. I sent him up to Centreville a while back. Told him to put the pedal on the floor going, then play it legal on the way back. You wouldn't believe the time he made."

"So he's Stirling Moss," McLeod said.

"Who?"

"Forget it. I don't want a kid on this."

"No?"

"No," McLeod snapped. "Dammit, he's gotta do more than drive. He's gotta be able to stand the gaff if the cops sweat him a little. He's gotta be able to hold together if guns go off. He's got to know how to keep his mouth shut. How old is he, anyway?"

"I never looked at his birth certificate, Marty."

"Burl—"

The fat man smiled. "You get excited," he said. "You get too excited. Maybe you should drink a little."

"A goddamn kid—"

"All we need him for is driving. All he gets is five gees, Marty. Not a full share, not close to a full share. You couldn't buy a better wheelman for that kind of money if you looked all over the world. He won't have a gun to use. He'll just sit in the car and drive like a sonofabitch."

"He's a kid."

"But he ain't like other kids. Tougher. And he can keep his trap shut."

"I don't like it," McLeod said.

"You don't have to," Burl told him.

They kicked it back and forth and Burl wound up on top, the way he always did. It was his show. They played around with a few more details and McLeod had a few more cups of coffee. Burl had another drink out of a fresh paper cup. He got up, lumbered out to his car and drove away. McLeod had more coffee.

Around seven he took the gun from his dresser drawer. The gun was a .38-caliber Smith & Wesson automatic, big enough to do the job and light enough to handle. It was the first gun he had ever owned, the only gun he had ever owned. He'd bought it recently at a hockshop in Cincinnati for fifty bucks over the counter with no questions asked. He picked up a box of ammunition at the same time.

He put the gun into a pocket, filled another pocket with shells. He went out the back door of the shack and walked down the road a few hundred yards, then cut across the field into a stand of poplar. He loaded the gun, sighted at a tree branch, squeezed the trigger. The slug was a full foot off the mark. He squeezed off another shot and hit the branch.

It was a warm night but a breeze was blowing, cooling the air a little, taking the edge off the humidity. He stayed out there for an hour and a half, practicing constantly with the pistol, pausing only to light cigarettes and to reload. The magazine carried seven shells. He got to shoot seven times before he had to load up again and start over.

He wasn't bad. At first he had been awful. The gun was new to him, it felt strange, and he always managed to jerk the gun just enough at the instant of firing to ruin his shots. Time and practice took care of that. He learned to sight precisely, to squeeze the shot off, to absorb the recoil of the gun with the muscles of his arm. He liked the gun and he liked practicing with it. You became a new man when you had a gun in your hand. It was strength, manhood, power.

He practiced every shot in the world. He didn't bother with fast draws—they were a Hollywood notion and he wouldn't need them. But he practiced shooting from a standing position, practiced sitting and supine and prone, practiced shooting while he was running forward or backward, to the left or to the right. That was important. You could be Dick Dead-Eye on the range and not show a thing in a pitched battle. It wasn't enough to be on the ball when you had all the time in the world. You had to be able to get the shots off fast; otherwise you were useless when it got rough.

Whatever illusions he had had at the beginning were gone now. The guards in the armored truck were going to die. That was the only way to play it. If they were left alive, they would be witnesses. You couldn't leave witnesses. So they had to die.

It didn't bother him. The robbery was part of a new life, and the values of the old life couldn't be a part of that new life. It was easier, maybe, if you fooled yourself about murder. You could plan a whole job and tell yourself that no one would be hurt in the course of it, and when you pulled the job you shot them all down and wrote it off as a shame. But he saw no reason to fool himself. The guards would die. That was a risk they signed on for when they took the job. To hell with them.

The kid, though. The kid bothered him more than the possible death of the guards. He didn't care how worldly Burl thought the kid was. There was a certain type of hardness that you couldn't develop on your own. It had to be pounded into you by life and the world. The kid—Jimmy something—had not lived long enough to acquire that sort of hardness.

McLeod knew what kids were like when they got mixed up in something big. He'd met kids like that at McAllister, and he had also met older cons who had gotten screwed up by letting themselves get involved with punk kids.

The kids did one of two things. They either fell apart, in which case they stooled afterward or balled things up beforehand, or else they got kill-happy. Either way you were in trouble. A scared kid and a kill-happy kid were both liabilities. McLeod didn't care how great a driver this kid was. He'd be happier with an older man at the wheel.

He finished off the last round of ammo, then broke the gun down and cleaned it. He hadn't had a woman or a really healthy drink since he made his choice. He didn't need either. Just coffee and target practice and food and sleep. That was all he needed. The job at the Land's End Cafe was over and done with. He had told the manager that he wouldn't be working any more, that night work was beginning to disagree with him and his eyes were going bad. So he had plenty of time to himself now, plenty of time to do whatever he wanted.

The kid still bothered him. Jimmy, Jimmy Kell, that was his name. The hotshot hotrod kid, the wheelman.

Well, the hell with him. If he was what Burl wanted, it looked as though they were stuck with him.

It was Burl's show.

Newport is in Kentucky, just across the Ohio River from Cincinnati. There is virtually no vice in Cincinnati and there is a very good reason for this. The reason is Newport, where there is all manner of vice, where everything is in operation right out in the open, and where a crackdown on prostitution and gambling would cripple the economic structure of the town.

Burl drove to Newport. Once a week, sure as God made little green virgins, Burl drove to Newport. There were plenty of whores in Indiana, but there were no full-fledged old-fashioned whorehouses, and there is a world of difference between a plain old round-heeled hooker and a Newport whorehouse whore.

Burl drove there, parked his car. He went into the Third Street Grille on Third Street just off Drumm Boulevard. They had an unusual arrangement for a whorehouse. The place was a luncheonette, complete with stools and coffee urn and Formica counter. The food was a little better than average.

But if you came just for food you would generally be asked politely to leave. The Third Street Grille did not particularly care whether or not it sold any food or coffee in the course of the day. What it sold, basically, was sex. When you walked through the luncheonette part of the operation you entered a parlor, where females were generally seated. When you selected one of these females and took her upstairs to a bedroom, you did not enter either a parlor or a luncheonette.

You entered a female.

Burl didn't order food. He walked into the lunchroom, smiled at the fat blonde who was overflowing one of the stools. She grinned at him, got to her feet, clapped him on the shoulder. "Good Old Charlie Ives," she bellowed. "Good to see you, you horny old son of a bitch!"

"Hello," he said. "Hello, Madge."

"Go on in there," Madge roared. "My girls are lonesome for you. Susie and Helen are there, and a girl you ain't ever seen yet. A redhead called Honey. Go have a time for yourself, you dirty old bastard!"

He went into the back room. The redhead, Honey, was a lovely young thing with a surprisingly innocent face. But he wasn't interested in her. Susie and Helen were also there, and Susie and Helen knew Burl and knew what he wanted. Old whores, like old friends and old wine and old shoes, are more to be trusted, more mellow, and more comfortable, in that metaphoric order. He took Susie by one arm and Helen by another and the three of them climbed the stairs and went into a room together. Susie closed the door, and Helen turned to Burl and smiled at him.

"The usual?"

"Well, now," he said. "You little girls want to think of anything new, why you just go right ahead. You know how to please an old man, don't you?"

They took off their clothes. Susie was a bottle blonde with the dark roots showing slightly. Unlike some peroxide aficionados, she had not troubled to bleach herself in every possible area. She was a tall girl, a little on the thin side, with very long legs and arms and a narrow waist. Her breasts, firm and spaced well apart, were medium in size.

Helen was a different type physically, short and dark and plump and cuddly. Her breasts were a little bit too large, but no one had ever objected to the fact. Helen was built for comfort, a warm brunette with a willing body. She got onto the bed, and Susie joined her, and Burl smiled.

"Well, now," he said. He dragged an overstuffed leather chair over next to the bed and eased his bulk into it. His eyes were on the two girls. "Well, now," he said again. "Well."

The girls went into their act. Helen lay down on her back while Susie made love to her, first kissing her on the mouth, then fondling her breasts. Then Helen began to come to life, reaching out to titillate Susie, stroking first her blonde hair and then elsewhere.

"Well, now," Burl said.

Susie found an artifact and put it to use. The artifact was a rather interesting one, cylindrical and long. The artifact was equipped with a harness apparatus, and Helen helped the bleached blonde strap the harness in place around her hips. Then, while Burl watched, the pair began to duplicate the approximate motions of heterosexual love.

"Well, now," Burl said. "Well."

For ten minutes, Burl sat and watched the two of them. They paid no apparent attention to him, which was fine as far as he was concerned. He watched, intent, his hands hanging upon the arms of the overstuffed leather chair, his eyes seeming to protrude slightly from his head. He watched, and when he had watched for some ten minutes his passion spent itself noiselessly and he rose just as noiselessly to his feet. Susie and Helen continued to have sex on the bed. They paid no attention to him. He took a crisp fifty-dollar bill from his wallet, placed it on the dresser, covered it with an ash tray so it would not blow away. Then he walked down the stairs and left the whorehouse.

Madge stared out after him, then sipped her cold coffee. "A fruitcake," she told the girl behind the counter. "Lives up in Indiana, makes his money peddling shine to the kooks up there. He comes down here like clockwork once a week and takes two of my girls upstairs. Never lays a hand on them."

"What does he do?"

"He watches," Madge said. "They go to bed, and he watches. Then he gets up and goes. Comes and goes, matter of fact. Leaves fifty bucks and goes. He's a goddamn watchbird."

*　　　*　　　*

Betty Marie sat in the front seat of the Pontiac convertible and looked out the window. Jimmy was in the hardware store buying something and she was waiting for him. She saw the man coming down the street, and she recognized him.

It was McLeod.

She had seen him before, when he was working at the Land's End Cafe. He didn't work there any more. According to Jimmy, he was in on the plan. She had asked about McLeod once, and Jimmy had grinned and told her that McLeod was in on the plan.

He wouldn't tell her what the plan was. He was like a little kid some of the time, she thought. The plan, whatever it was, was a deep dark secret, a hidden secret that he could not share with her. But he wasn't man enough to keep it secret and forget it when he was with her. He obviously wanted to tell her about it, because he kept hinting at it, kept teasing her with it. Like a baby, like a little kid.

McLeod wasn't a little kid. She saw him pass the Pontiac and continue on down the street, walking quickly and firmly, his arms swinging at his sides. McLeod wouldn't play games like that. McLeod was tough, strong.

She wondered what it would be like with McLeod.

There was a way to find out, a very simple way. All she had to do was go to McLeod and ask him to take her to bed. But she had a strong feeling that it might not work. McLeod wasn't the kind of man who would jump out of his pants just because a woman was willing to go to bed with him. He'd probably laugh at her and tell her to get lost. Maybe he'd tell her to stick to punk kids her own age, something like that.

She didn't want kids her own age.

She wanted a man.

In a sense, there was nothing wrong with Jimmy. But if you are not genuinely in love with a lover, familiarity can only breed contempt. You begin to see flaws, and the flaws are not the components of a lovable personality but weak points in a structure, and with the passage of time the flaws become progressively more of a nuisance.

This was happening with Jimmy. She still spent a lot of time with him, and she still wound up on a blanket with him whenever given the opportunity, and she still swigged shine from the bottle with him and had sex with him and went on a joyride to Jupiter with him. But it was not the same as it had been at first, and it was getting further and further from that state every day, and she didn't really want him any more.

She wanted McLeod.

The hardware store door opened. Jimmy came out, carrying a brown paper bag in one hand. It looked heavy. He grinned at her, walked around the car, opened the trunk, tossed the bag inside. It made a clanking sound. He closed the trunk and locked it, then walked around the car and got behind the wheel.

"Hi," he said. "Sorry if I kept you waiting."

"It's all right."

He stuck the key in the ignition. "Well," he said, "let's roll out of here."

They rolled out of there, leaving their usual rubber patch behind them on the pavement. In time, she thought, the tires on the Pontiac convertible would be thin as tissue paper. At first he had excited her by peeling out of parking spaces. Now she thought it was childish.

She asked him where they were going.

"On an afternoon as hot as this one? Swimming."

"Where?"

"The quarry."

"Nobody goes there any more," she said. "Not since that boy drowned a year ago. The place is deserted."

He winked at her. "That's the whole idea," he said.

The quarry was actually more of a gravel pit than a real rock quarry. A company dredged sand and gravel from it, leaving a deep pit that filled with spring water. The sides of the pit were steep, and when you went into the quarry there was a quick drop-off that could get you if you didn't know how to swim. There had been a drowning there the previous summer, and the gravel company had placed the quarry off-limits to swimmers. Jimmy drove there, pushing the convertible, squealing to a stop on the private road that ran to the quarry. The dredgers were not there, and there were no other prospective swimmers on hand. They had the place to themselves.

"Come on," he said, getting out of the car. "Let's hit that water, girl!"

She peeled off her clothes at the water's edge, stripped herself naked and stood for a moment at the edge of the pit. Jimmy was nude, and it occurred to her how genuinely ridiculous a nude man looked at any time other than during the sex act. He looked foolish. She giggled at him, and he reached over to slap her on the buttocks. She charged him, jumped at him. He dodged and she went sprawling in the sand and he burst out laughing at her.

"Go ahead and laugh," she snapped. "You don't know what can happen if that sand goes in the wrong place!"

He went on laughing. She ran at him, shoved him. He sprawled into the water, then started swimming. She went in after him. The water was ice-cold and chilled her to the bone. She chased him across the quarry, knifing through the water with crisp strokes, catching him finally and throwing her arms around his neck. She ducked him and came up gurgling.

"Let's do it," she said.

He stared at her.

"Right here," she said. "Let's make love in the water, Jimmy. Come on!"

"It's impossible," he said. "We would drown."

"Don't be silly," she said. "We could sort of tread water, see, and we could—"

They tried, in a way. But it didn't work out at all. Once they wound up sinking below the surface of the water. His hands were on her breasts and his mouth was glued to her mouth, and for a horrible moment she thought that they *would* drown there, that they would quietly sink in one another's arms to the bottom of the quarry and stay there until the flesh came loose from their bones.

This didn't happen. They surfaced, spat out water, and

swam together for shore. She waited at the water's edge while he got the old familiar blanket from the trunk and spread it on the sand. Then she joined him and he took her in his arms.

When he kissed her, it suddenly occurred to her how she could meet McLeod.

She didn't worry about it right then, however. She had other things to do, and she devoted all of her attention to them. They were important things, all things considered, and they were things at which she had become surprisingly adept, and she wasn't going to worry about McLeod while she was doing them.

It was nice. Her whole body was wringing wet, and he was stroking her wet breasts with his wet hands, and rubbing her wet thighs with his wet fingers, and it was so delicious she wanted to shout. And then, when his strong young body was between her pulsating thighs, it was even better. She rocked and rolled and bucked and wailed, and her heart did a somersault and her insides turned upside-down, and there was a private and delightful earthquake between her legs.

Afterward she swam a while, then came out of the water and stretched out beside him on the blanket. He was curled up on his side, eyes closed, letting the sun dry him. She curled next to him and kissed his eyelids.

"Jimmy," she said.

He didn't answer her.

"Jimmy, tell me about the job."

One eye opened. He looked at her curiously.

"The job you and McLeod and Burl are planning."

He winked the one eye. "Hell," he said, "I can't tell you a thing like that."

"Please?"

"Can't do it."

She sighed. "It's probably a big deal, all right. You'll rob a blind newsboy or something. You make it sound important, but I'll bet it's nothing at all."

"That's what you think, honey."

"If it was really important," she said, playing her trump card, "they wouldn't let a kid like you in on it."

She got the reaction she wanted, of course. And she had to fight to keep the grin from appearing on her face. She listened quietly and carefully while he told her about the job, and she prompted him from time to time with little questions that would draw him out, and bit by bit she got every last detail out of him. He was proud as a peacock while he told her. He felt very important. A real big deal, she thought. They were just letting him drive. He wasn't one of the big shots.

But he told her everything she wanted to know, and it was plenty. Now she wouldn't have any trouble getting McLeod to listen to her.

And after that it would be easy.

Chapter 6

The young widow on Walnut Street was named Sandra Craig. She was twenty-six, and she had been a widow for two years, ever since her husband had been devoured by a jet plane. Her husband was a man named Rudy Craig, and he had been in the air force at the time, putting in a few years as a ground crew type. A jet had been idling at the time, and Rudy had managed to walk too close in front of it, and the intake had sucked him in and ever since that unhappy day Sandra Craig had been a widow.

She was a pretty girl, chesty and leggy, with a heart-shaped face and a pointed chin and ice-blue eyes. She taught third grade at the Cedar Corners grade school, lived alone, and had little to say to anyone. She never dated, although the mourning period had ended some time ago.

Luke figured he couldn't miss. A hot young broad, all alone for two years. Married first, accustomed to getting it steady, and then out of it since then. She's be starving, he told himself. She'd beg for it.

It was just getting to be night when he rang her bell. The sky was growing dark, and the moon was a fat orange ball lying close to the horizon, bright and beautiful against the purple sky. He leaned on the bell, waited for her to answer it. A cigarette dangled nonchalantly from one corner of his mouth. One hand was on his hip, the other at his side.

Sandra Craig opened the door.

"Hello," he said. "Hello, teacher."

She looked at him. He looked back, letting his eyes roam over her lush young body. Breasts poked out at him from beneath a sleeveless blouse the color of starchy corn. Legs swelled under a pearl gray skirt. He pushed past her, went into her house. She turned automatically and followed him, her eyes wide, her mouth open.

Nice, he thought. He had her buffaloed now. She didn't know what was happening, and that was just fine. By the time she found out her legs would be wide apart and he'd be between them, filling her hips with boys and girls.

Nice.

"I don't know you," she said.

"Luke," he said. "Luke Penner."

"I don't—"

She let the words hang there, left the sentence unfinished. He didn't help her out. Instead he just looked at her, giving her the full bedroom glare that she couldn't misinterpret. She didn't misinterpret it. She blushed, and she tried to turn her eyes away.

She didn't make it.

"I was thinking about you," he said.

"You were?"

"Uh-huh."

"I—"

"I was thinking about you, Teacher. I was thinking that there was something you needed."

"What?"

"To get laid," he said.

For a moment everything simply stopped. The word shattered the evening into shards of broken time, and Sandra Craig stared at him with glassy eyes, and the world stopped. It stood quite still, and he watched her, holding his composure together and hoping it would go right. He wanted her now. He'd wanted a lot of girls lately, and he'd had a lot of them, but this was different. This was a test. If you could score with the widow schoolmarm you could score with anybody in the world.

And he wanted to score. He looked at her breasts, shaped to fit a man's hand, and he looked at her hips, generously made for childbirth and child-conception, and he wanted her. She was waiting, motionless, trying to fit together enough words to speak, and he stepped up close to her and grinned.

"Too long," he said softly. "You've been too long without a man, teacher. You need it more than I do, and I need it bad enough myself. So you just come here, teacher, and Luke'll show you just what you been missing too long."

There was a moment there when she could have resisted. If she had taken a step back just then, and if she had laughed at him or cursed him or mocked him, she would have won. She did none of these things. Instead she stood in place, frozen, a statue, while he took her in his arms and covered her mouth with his.

Then it was too late.

He kissed her, squeezing her good female body tight against his, feeling the breasts press against him and the hips warm to him. He worked his mouth against hers, parted her lips with his tongue, tasted the infinite sweetness of her mouth. And, magically, she began to respond to him. First was returning the kiss, sedately but perceptibly, and then she was returning the embrace, holding him, hugging him.

He had it made.

He wanted to holler, to shout out the story of his success to the world. But it was no time to shout. It was a time to stroke the back of her neck with sensitive fingers, a time to lift her gently in his arms and carry her quickly to her bedroom. There was a double bed in the room, a bed that had held only one person for far too long. He dropped her on the bed and fell beside her, grabbed her, kissed her.

She took off her blouse, then stopped and fell back limp on her pillow. She didn't move while he stripped her naked, peeling off bra and skirt and panties and stockings and tossing everything in a tired heap on the floor. He looked at her. She was a statue now. Her eyes were closed, her limbs limp. She was naked and beautiful and the seat of his manhood throbbed with desire for her.

He took off his clothes. Then he hesitated. There were two ways to do it now. He could work on her slowly, deliberately, building up her passion an inch at a time until she screamed her need at the sky. Or he could take her quickly, brutally, slamming her and belting her with lust while she lay as motionless as she could, until finally the need reached her and she turned into a wildcat.

He settled on the first way.

It was more of a challenge.

Slowly, then. His hands on her shoulders, his mouth on her mouth. He kissed her and she did not kiss back. His hands on her breasts then, stroking, fondling. She didn't respond, but he grinned as her breasts warmed to his touch and her nipples grew hard as pink diamonds. Go ahead and play it cool, he thought. Those nipples give you away, teacher.

He put his mouth to her breast, planted a trail of kisses on the montizorous mound of flesh. His tongue darted out, drawing circles around the breast, circles that grew progressively smaller as they came closer and closer to the tip. Then he had his mouth around the nipple. He bit her, hard enough to bring tears to her eyes, and then he was kissing the nipple and she was beginning to breath hard, the blood pounding through her body.

Nice.

Very nice.

She did scream, finally. He teased her for half an hour, doing everything to her but the final thing, and she screamed at him. She told him what she wanted, and she told him in no uncertain terms. Her terms, as a matter of fact, were about as certain as you could get. They were not what you might be justified in expecting from a third-grade teacher. They were gutter terms and she used them like a gutter tramp.

She told him what to take, and she told him where to put it, and she told him what to do to her, and the bulk of her bedroom vocabulary was composed of four-letter words. She screamed, and she begged, and she pleaded, and then he went into her the way the Wehrmacht went into Poland in '39 and she stopped using words and screamed syllables of pain and pleasure and lust.

He drove her wild. He kept her busy half the night, and when he left her she was unable to move. She was too weak, too tired, too almost dead. Her arms were heavy as lead and her legs were heavy as platinum and her breasts were sore and her body ached with the good sweet ache of overexertion. She slept for ten hours without moving.

When she woke up, joints aching and muscles sore, she realized what she had said and what she had done.

She cried like a baby.

Betty Marie sat at the counter at the Land's End Cafe. She was smoking a cigarette and drinking a cup of coffee and listening idly to the jukebox. The afternoon was another hot one. In the morning it had rained, and everybody told everybody else how the rain would be good for the farmers, and nobody really gave a loose damn deep down inside whether the rain was good for the farmers or not. Around noon the rain stopped, and the sun came out, and it was hotter than ever, all of which was distinctly bad for the farmers. So people stopped talking about farmers one way or the other and went on sweating again.

Betty Marie wasn't sweating. She dropped her cigarette on the floor, covered it with a foot which was in turn covered by a white tennis sneaker. She ground out the cigarette and thought about five men who were going to rob an armored car.

It was one hell of a deal. She hadn't been prepared for anything that big, not when she started pumping Jimmy for the lowdown on it. If it was really big, she had thought, they wouldn't want Jimmy in on it. But at the same time it had to be fairly significant or McLeod wouldn't waste his time on it.

It was bigger than she had suspected. One hundred thousand dollars, give or take a little. Five thousand for Jimmy, since he was really not much more than a hired hand. That left a lot of money to be split between four men.

She sipped her coffee. Now was the time, she thought. Now she had a way to reach McLeod. He couldn't ignore her, not when she came on strong with news like that. He'd fall over when she told him. He'd have a goddamned stroke.

She was lighting a fresh cigarette when it occurred to her that a few months ago she might have gone on the run to the police with the news. Such a course of action hardly entered her mind now. She had changed. And the change had to be something a good deal deeper than a loss of virginity. You could attribute a certain amount of change to the absence of a square inch or so of membranous tissue, but not everything. She had changed greatly; her whole moral outlook was radically different.

She needed excitement, needed it the way a drug addict needs heroin. She needed to be alive, dynamically alive, and that need overshadowed the sort of moral code that had been her birthright. So she didn't even consider going to the police. The police represented the status quo, the normal order of things, and she was standing on the opposite side of every fence in the world from them. She was not interested in preserving the status quo. She wanted thrills, movement, dynamism, and that put her on the side of Jimmy and Burl and McLeod.

McLeod.

She finished her coffee, paid for it, left the Land's End. It was a fairly long walk to the shack where McLeod was living, an even longer walk in that heat. She managed it, stopping from time to time to wipe the sweat from her forehead. By the time she reached McLeod's shack she was too tired to stand up. She knocked on his door. When he opened it she pushed past him and sank into a chair.

"Okay," he said. "Who the hell are you?"

"Betty Marie James."

"So?"

She looked at him. Tough, she thought. Hard, all the way through. You could stick out your tits at McLeod and it wouldn't move him. He didn't move easy.

"I need a drink," she said.

"There's nothing around."

"Water, then."

He filled a tumbler with cold tap-water and handed it to her. She drained it in a single swallow, set it down empty on top of an orange-crate bookcase.

"McLeod," she said, "I want you."

He laughed at her. She blushed, and he broke off the laughter and pointed to the door.

"Get out," he said.

"McLeod—"

"Come back in a few years," he said. "If you live to be eighteen, come around then. Get out, jailbait."

"I thought jailbait was what you used to catch jailbirds."

He walked over, slapped her once. The blow rocked her head back and made her dizzy. She put her hand to her face. Her face hurt from the slap.

"Out," he said.

"So I'm jailbait," she said. "So I'm just a kid. There are compensations, McLeod."

"Listen—"

"I'm firm," she said. "Really firm." She cupped her breasts with her hands, held them out to him. "Firm as melons," she said. "Isn't that something?"

"Congratulations."

"And something else," she said. "It comes with being young, McLeod. I'm tight."

"More congratulations."

"Really tight," she went on, smiling inside. "McLeod, I'm as tight as an armored truck."

He slapped her, then. He was next to her in a minute,

hauling her up out of the chair with one hand, slapping her forehead and backhand with the other. The slaps knocked her senseless, and when he let go of her she went sprawling to the floor. She got up slowly, dazed.

"Talk," he said.

"I came to talk," she told him. "You didn't have to hit me."

"Dammit—"

She talked hurriedly. "I'm Jimmy Kell's girl," she said. "He told me. He was bragging about it to me one day after he screwed me at the quarry. He was boasting, telling me what a big shot he was. I thought you might want to know about it, McLeod."

McLeod was pacing the floor, smacking one fist into the palm of his other hand. "The little bastard," he said. "We needed that little bastard like a hole in the head. That rotten stupid big-mouthed little bastard—"

"Are you glad I came, McLeod?"

He turned to her. "Yeah," he said. "Sure."

"I could have gone to the cops. Instead I came to you."

"To blackmail me? It'd be easier to kill you than pay you, sweetheart."

"Not for blackmail."

"Then why?"

She stood up, moved toward him. This was the right kind of man, she thought. The kind you had to work for, the kind who didn't shake in his pants just because you grinned at him.

"I told you," she said.

He didn't say anything.

"I said I wanted you," she went on. "I still want you, McLeod."

He didn't really want her, not just then. All he gave a damn about was the job and all he wanted to do was make sure the stupid bastard Jimmy Kell didn't blow the deal ahead of time. He didn't care about the broad. She was a broad, a good-to-look-at broad, but that was all she was.

He didn't particularly want her. But she was there, itching to get laid, and he had to do something to keep her quiet for the time being. He had a choice between fucking her and killing her. Killing her was murder, and for that they electrocuted you. Fucking her was statutory rape, and for that they gave you five-to-twenty. The answer was obvious.

He took off his clothes. She watched him for a moment, then began to undress. As her clothes disappeared his desire began to grow. A good body, he saw. A girl's face and a whore's heart and a woman's body, and you couldn't ask for a better combination than that.

When he touched her, he was not caressing her, not trying to excite her. He handled her breasts as a peasant housewife handles fruit at the market, testing them, squeezing them, noting the resiliency and the size and the feel of them. He dumped her on the bed, still without a caress, and he fell on her like a horse, and he took her, stabbed her, pierced her, and it began to be as it had never been before.

"McLeod—"

Her voice was tense, electric. He sank his teeth into her shoulder, choking off her words, and he sank into her, drew forth, plunged. She was the first woman he had taken in his shack and he was baptizing the place with her sweet underage body. The bed wailed—it was an old army cot, not built for such exercise. It screeched in ageless rhythm and his body and her body moved like magic, sweating and straining in the heat of the afternoon, spreading out the world and burying mountains and filling valleys and driving the sun out of the sky.

Long ago, before his whore wife had opened her legs to another man, it had been like this. Not just a pair of bodies, not just sex, but something bigger and infinitely better. Since then he had forgotten what it could be like. He had drunk and fornicated with Joyce Ramsdell, and he had tricked himself into thinking that there was nothing more than that, and that a man could get along without it.

Wrong.

Double-wrong.

Because this was it, this was the real thing, this was flesh hungry for flesh and body seeking body and the world turning over and spilling itself dry. This was it, this was how it had to be, how it could only be.

Perfect.

Better than perfect.

With thunder and lightning, with clouds and a storm,

with starbursts and violins and trumpets and volcanoes. With everything, the whole works inside and out and up and down and top to bottom and east to west and north to south, all of it, nothing held back, everything there.

All.

Bells ringing, bombs exploding. All of it. Her voice screaming fulfillment, her nails raking his back, drawing rivers of blood. His teeth in her shoulder biting off a scream of his own. All of it. Everything.

Then, at last, silence as flat as a grave.

Afterward, they slept. Neither of them moved for two hours, and their sweat merged while they slept, and there was silence. He awoke first, felt her body in his arms, remembered. He didn't open his eyes. He didn't have to—he read her body by Braille, and he stroked her and woke her with his hands, and then they merged again. She was only half awake while they made love. It was animalish, out of sleep and into sex, and it was perfect.

They took showers, dried off, got dressed. He lighted two cigarettes and gave one of them to her. She sucked smoke down into her lungs, blew it out. She smiled at him and he winked at her and she touched his chest with one of her small hands.

"McLeod," she said.

"I guess I'm stuck with you," he told her.

"Forever."

"Something like that."

"Until we're both dead, McLeod. That's two lifetimes from now."

"Yeah."

"What do we do, McLeod?"

"About what?"

"The truck. The robbery."

He thought it over, working on his cigarette, focusing his eyes on the floor of the shack. He was fairly sure the Kell kid hadn't told anybody else. He could move in on her now, tell the kid that Betty Marie was his woman and the kid should go back to jerking off.

But that could be messy. The kid was a punk, dumb enough to make trouble, young enough to be a pain in the ass. It would be easier to let the kid think everything was the way it had been. Let Betty Marie be the kid's exclusive piece of tail, at least as far as he was concerned. Let him find out later, or never.

"We handle the job the same way," he said.

"And Jimmy?"

"You stay with him."

"You're tired of me already, McLeod?"

She made a joke out of it; she knew it wasn't true. "You tell him you've got your period," he said. "It's a week until we pull it off. Don't let him near you for that week. I don't want the little prick touching you."

"Neither do I."

"Don't let him know anything happened. Let him think you didn't see me and you didn't say a word to me."

"Right."

"Once we hit that truck, then the kid can go to hell. It's you and me for a long time. You know that, don't you?"

"I know."

He put out his cigarette. "There's more," he said. "I figured I'd have to get a long ways out of town once we pulled this off. As soon as Burl told me we were letting the kid in on it, I knew he'd talk sooner or later. You have to expect it of a punk like Kell. As soon as the job's done, we get a long ways out of Cedar Corners."

"Good."

"And out of Indiana. A long ways across the state line. Once we're over the line, it'll be that much harder for them to get to us. You understand that?"

"I understand."

He drew a breath. "There'll be Feds in on it," he said. "An armored car is the same as a bank. A Federal offense. They'll have the FBI in on the thing, so they won't let go once we're over the state line. But it'll make it tougher for them. And they won't know exactly what to look for, either. We'll have a lot of money, Betty Marie."

"How much?"

"Twenty grand," he said. "Maybe more."

"More?"

He looked away. "Maybe," he said. He thought about it, then shrugged it off for the time being. That was something he could always worry about later. Not now.

"Listen," he said, "we'll cut west. The coast, California. Then maybe down to Mexico if it stays hot. You know how you can live in Mexico on money like that?"

"Tell me."

"Like a king and a queen," he said. "Think you can stand it, kitten? No more Cedar Corners?"

"I hate this town, McLeod."

"I like it better today than I did yesterday."

"The only thing I like about it is that you're in it, McLeod."

He reached for her, kissed her. She burrowed her face into his chest, cuddling up like a kitten. This one wouldn't cheat, he told himself. This one couldn't cheat. Even if she put out for somebody else, it wouldn't be cheating because nobody could reach her the way he reached her. Nobody else could give her what he had given her. He didn't have to worry, not about this one.

"We'll make it," she said. "Won't we?"

"Sure."

"Cops and FBI men. They'll be after us."

"We'll get away."

"Will there be killing, McLeod?"

There were girls you lied to and there were girls you levelled with. She was the kind that could handle the truth.

"Probably."

"Will you kill anybody?"

"Probably."

"And if they catch us?"

"Then we're dead. I am, anyway. You'll go to jail. I don't think you'd like jail, kitten."

"I won't go, McLeod. They'll have to kill me too."

He kissed her again. Desire rose, suddenly, without

warning. It was amazing. He wanted her in a new way, and it was good.

And she wanted him, too. "Forget about killing," she said, her voice husky. "Let's make some more love, McLeod."

Chapter 7

Jimmy Kell was there to meet them at the airport. He picked up Mike Lieber on a Monday, in the morning, with the job just five days away. He got up early in the morning, around seven, wolfed down a fast breakfast and hopped behind the wheel of the Pontiac convertible. He put the accelerator on the floor and pointed the car toward Rushville. The plane landed on schedule at Rushville Airport and a tall, thin man got off it. His shoulders were hunched, his brow furrowed. He was partially bald. He wore a pair of pin-stripe slacks and a matching vest but no jacket. From the description, he had to be Mike Lieber.

Jimmy went to him. "Burl sent me," he said. "You Mike?"

Lieber nodded.

"Want a hand with those?"

"No."

"They look heavy—"

Lieber was carrying a briefcase and a guitar case. In the briefcase he had two clean shirts, three suits of underwear, a book on how to beat the horses, and a .45-caliber pistol. In the guitar case he had a sub-machine gun, several rounds of ammunition for it, and enough old rags to keep everything from rattling around. He told Jimmy the bags weren't heavy, and that they should get into the car and go. They got into the Pontiac and they went.

"You can talk to me," Jimmy said. "I mean I'm not just some hired hand or something."

Mike Lieber grunted.

"I'm part of the party. I'm wheeling, you know? I'm doing the driving."

Mike Lieber didn't grunt. He didn't speak, either. Jimmy managed to dope out the fact that Mike wasn't interested in talking, or in being talked to, and he stopped trying.

That was Monday. Lieber went to Burl's place and talked with him—or listened to him—for an hour. Then he walked over to the house of a woman who took in roomers. He rented a room, signing the register *John Martin*. He had his briefcase with him; the guitar case stayed with Burl.

That was Monday. Tuesday Jimmy drove again to the airport, in the afternoon this time. He picked up Jack Dawes. Dawes was as heavy as Mike Lieber was thin, as loud as Lieber was silent. He hit Jimmy on the shoulder, grinned at him, and piled himself heavily into the Pontiac. He was a wide man, with cauliflower ears and a nose that had been broken more than a few times and that had been improperly reset at least twice. He had a single airlines flight bag and nothing else. The bag contained two handguns and a variety of rumpled clothing. He set the bag down on the floorboards at his feet and relaxed.

"You," he said to Jimmy. "What's your end of this?"

"I drive."

"Yeah, Burl was saying. Ever been in one of these before, kid?"

"No."

"Jesus," Jack Dawes said. "I remember one time in Milwaukee, me and Eddie Hart and Lou the Screw. We took the loan company, walked in on the shylocks with guns showing and walked out with a bagful of dough and there's a cop standing there with his gun drawn. That was a lulu, kid."

"What happened?"

"What happened?" Jack burlesqued a shrug. "He killed us all," he said. "Kid, he killed every last one of us. It was a fucking bloodbath, kid."

Jimmy colored. Jack Dawes slapped him on the back, laughed uproariously. "A joke," he said. "Just a joke, kid. To sort of ease you up for the job."

Jimmy drove him to Burl's house. Burl gave him a pint of shine and a room to drink it in, and Jack Dawes went up to his room and killed the pint and went to sleep.

That was Tuesday. Jimmy looked around for Betty Marie later on that day, found her, took her driving. The tension was beginning to build now. He could feel it. Everybody who was in on the thing was reacting to it in one way or another. Burl snapped orders brusquely, didn't hear questions, brooded. McLeod had been cutting him dead, and Jimmy couldn't figure out what the big man had against him, or whether he was just tight as a bowstring about everything. Mike Lieber was silent, but the word had it that Iron Mike was silent about everything, so that didn't seem to be too significant. Jack Hawes was loose and easy, joking and back-slapping and loud, and Jimmy decided that he was either the coolest man who ever drew breath or else this was his way of concealing and overpowering his fears.

Jimmy had a different reaction. It was a need, a big blind need that overshadowed everything.

A need for a woman.

And it didn't do any good. He could need all day, and for all the good it did him with Betty Marie he might as well have gone and castrated himself. Thirty days in a month, and she had to pick the week before the job to come down with the curse. Thirty days in a month, and she had to pick these days to fly the red flag. Dammit to hell!

It was his own fault, he thought. He should have knocked her up, and then there wouldn't have been any monthly problem like this. And he wasn't going to have much use for her after the job had been pulled. Maybe one quick piece for old time's sake, and then he'd be gone like the wind and she could stay behind and rot in Cedar Corners. He'd be across the state line with all of Indiana after him for armed robbery. What could she do, charge him with abandonment? Sue him for child support?

He drove around that afternoon, talking about this and that to ease the tension. He dropped her off before dinner and took a run up to Paulling to grab a meal. They had a place there that gave you a good steak for a buck and a half with home fries and coffee tossed in. He told them to make the steak well done and they almost burned it. He stuffed himself, drank a few cups of coffee, and got out of there.

The evening was a bastard—hot, breezeless. He spent most of it looking for a broad and not finding one. There was nothing in Paulling. He went back to the Corners, bought a few beers at the Land's End, waited for something to turn up. Nothing turned up. He gave up, finally, and went home.

He made love to his hand and went to sleep.

Luke liked the set-up.

He hadn't figured on it, not at first. He had gone after Sandra Craig because she was a broad who looked as though she'd be wild in the rack. Period. He figured on a quick score and a thank-you-ma'am and onward to greener pastures. The world was filled with tail, you only had to look to find it, and he didn't figure on saddling himself with one broad for any length of time. Spread it around, give 'em enough to make 'em know how sweet it is, and that's plenty.

He changed his mind.

He was standing on the street corner now, rolling a cigarette, twisting the ends. He snapped a match into flame and lighted the cigarette. It burned quickly; he had packed it a little too loosely. In a few long drags it was gone. He tossed the butt into the gutter and started walking to Walnut Street.

She lived on Walnut, of course. And it was night, and he always went to her at night. Once a night, every night, he went to see Sandra Craig.

She was never glad to see him. She was always rather miserable about it, and she didn't try to hide it, and that was where the tremendous kick came. Each and every night he leaned on her bell until she answered it, and each time he pushed her inside and closed the door, and each time she whimpered horribly and asked him to leave. But he didn't leave. Instead he would stand there, talking dirty to her, telling her what he had in his pants and how much she was itching for it.

Each night it was rape. A verbal rape first, with him coaxing and taunting and with her begging, pleading. And then a physical rape, because although she needed it and wanted it more than he did, she always put up a token fight to ease her conscience. And he loved that token fight. He loved overpowering her, loved carrying her into the bedroom, loved stuffing her full of cock until, at longest last, her protests stopped and her whimpers turned to shrieks of lust and she screamed her passion through the roof.

He loved it.

He went to her door now. The lights were on in her house, it was early, she was awake. He leaned on the bell, as usual, and he waited until the door opened.

"Please," she said.

He laughed, pushing her backward, coming inside and drawing the door shut. Damn, he thought. Ought to take her outside and screw her on the front lawn so the neighbors can watch. Well, some day he'd have to try it that way. Be good for a laugh or two, wouldn't it?

"Hello, teacher," he drawled. "Bought you an apple down at the store. Apple for the teacher."

"Please," she said.

"Glad to see me?"

"No."

"No?"

"I wish you would go away," she said. "I wish you would stay away and leave me alone."

He chuckled then broke it off, reaching out a hand to flick her breasts. No bra, he noted. That tipped her hand now, didn't it? She wanted him to go away, but she went braless to make things simpler for him.

"Apples for the teacher," he said again. "Teacher's got a few nice apples of her own. Big juicy pink apples with cherries for the tips. Like this, teacher?"

She shrank away from him, but not before he had cupped both breasts and had given them a squeeze. Firm flesh, lush and warm, sweet and lovely.

"You're the teacher," he said reflectively, "but I'm the one's got to give you a lesson. You like the kind of lessons you get from me, teacher? Better than they give you in third grade?"

She had stopped saying *please*. Now she was begging him with her eyes, asking him to leave, praying he would let her alone. Time to get a little rough, he thought. Time to knock old teacherina around a little. The cave men had the right idea, by God. Slap the crap out of a broad and it taught her how to behave.

"Teacher," he said, "let's have a party."

She sensed what was coming. She backed away from him, moved backward while he stalked her like a cat after a broken-winged robin. He caught her when she backed up against the wall, and it was comical to see her trying to shrink through the wall. She couldn't make it.

He hit her in the stomach.

It was a good punch, clean and solid. His fist sank deep into her belly and she let out a sick moan and doubled up. He drew back his hand, palm open, and he slapped her full force across the face. Her head bobbed back and glanced off the wall, making an odd thunking sound, and when she looked at him her eyes were glazed.

He didn't really mean to hit her in the breast. She had gorgeous knockers, and it was a shame to hurt them, but the punch he aimed at her belly came in too high and caught her flush in the breast. Her groan went through him like a knife. She sank to her knees and moaned awfully.

"Okay," he said. "That's enough, teacher."

He carried her into the bedroom and stripped her. Beautiful, he thought. A perfect body. One breast had a black-and-blue mark from the punch she had taken there, and he ran his fingertips across the mark. You been branded, he thought. That shows the world that you're Luke Penner's private stock.

"I hurt you," he said. "Didn't I?"

A whisper. "Yes."

"You hate me, don't you?"

"I wish you were dead."

"But you can't live without me, can you?"

No answer.

"Can't" he said. "You need it a hell of a lot more 'n I do, teacher. You itch for it. I could walk out and find some other pussy in a minute and never give you a thought again, but it would plain kill you. You burn for it."

She stared at him, hating him. He liked to see that particular expression in her eyes. The idea that she could hate him so much and need him so much, both at once, was exhilarating, It gave him a tremendous feeling of power.

"Do you want it now, teacher?"

"I want you to go away."

He covered the injured breast with a hand, squeezed hard enough to bring tears to her eyes. He squeezed again, and he saw passion join the pain, and he knew he had her where he wanted her.

"Go ahead," he said, his voice oddly gentle now. "Tell me to go away, teacher."

She tried. She tried very hard, but she couldn't say the words. They stuck in her throat.

"Then tell me what you really want, teacher."

She told him. She told him, and he got out of his clothes, and he tore at her and raped her. It wasn't a rape in the sense that she asked for it, that she wanted it, but once he was upon her she began to fight him tooth and nail. She fought knowing she would lose and hoping she would lose, and he knew this, and that made it all the better. He fought her and he beat her, and at the end she was loving it, loving all of it, moving of it and with it and for it and being moved by it, biting him and clawing at him and urging him on, deeper and deeper and harder and harder and faster and faster and oh God God God yes God yes damn yes yes yes—

"Teacher," he said, dressing, rolling a cigarette, turning to leave. "Teacher, you know what you are?"

No answer.

"You're just a pussy," he said. "And I own you, body and soul."

He paused at the door. She was crying audibly and he grinned from ear to ear. Then he opened the door and went out into the night, happy.

The five of them at Burl's house. Burl in his big chair, gesturing with a cigar that smelled worse than Burl did. Mike Lieber sitting stolid, nodding now and then. Jack Dawes working gingerly on a bottle of shine. Jimmy Kell chewing on a fingernail and trying not to look nervous.

McLeod sat and watched them. Of all of them, he alone felt completely calm. Mike and Jack were professionals and they didn't let their nervousness show but McLeod could feel it in the air, an electric network of jumping nerves.

McLeod wasn't nervous. It would go fine and he would be rich, or it would turn sour and he would be dead, and either way he was satisfied. If he died in it, too bad but all right. Because you could measure a life in years, or in a way that made more sense to McLeod. What counted was the amount of living you did. And he'd be doing more living by pulling the job than by stretching out the years in Cedar Corners.

There was a way to do still more living.

He looked around the little group. Burl was explaining something he had heard too many times already. He looked at Mike Lieber and Jack Dawes. They were getting twenty grand each from the operation. The kid—Jimmy—was in for five. McLeod was due to get twenty-five. The rest, less the expenses he was paying out of pocket, went to Burl. Thirty thousand, maybe a little more.

McLeod looked at his hands. He could have his twenty-five thou or he could have the whole bundle. That was the choice. It was something to consider, something to ponder until the wheels clicked and you knew which way to go.

He and Betty Marie could go a long way on twenty-five thou. They could go further on a hundred.

Something to think about.

"Let's take it from the top," Burl was saying. "The truck hits the outskirts of Centreville at 9:15 in the morning. That's when they reach the spot where we're hitting them. It takes two hours and forty minutes of safe-speed driving for us to get there from here. The boy timed it. Worked it out perfectly. If we hit the road at 6:30 we'll get there just about right."

Mike Lieber nodded.

"We drop Mike there on the ground. He hits the dirt by the side of the road they're coming down, and he has a chopper. Then we backtrack in the car so that we can be coming up while the truck is coming toward us. The truck gets to Mike, and he goes for the tires with the chopper. That sends them toward us and we hit them hard."

McLeod tapped the floor rhythmically with his left foot. He saw it all clearly, easily. Mike would hit them from the side, sending the armored vehicle spinning. The guards would come out with guns ready, and the convertible would be there to give them a lead-bath. Jack Dawes would have a handgun and so would McLeod. Burl would be spraying with the second chopper. The guards were going to get shot dead as doornails, and nobody was keeping this a secret any more. The pitch about maybe-they'll-surrender had been discarded a while ago.

Once the guards were down it was easy. Open up the back, grab the money bags, flip them into the Pontiac's trunk. Swing around, pick up Mike, head for home. Take it slow or fast on the way back, all depending upon how it went during the job itself. If it was smooth and there were no clues left, take it easy and stick to the speed limit. If not, let the driver earn his five grand.

McLeod liked it. It beat a lot of set-ups. The standard routine involved cutting off the truck with the car, forcing him to stop. That could be a hang-up. For one thing, the truck could remember the fact that it was bigger than a car, in which case it didn't stop at all. It plowed right into you and killed you then and there.

That happened once in a while. More likely, the truck stopped and the guards came up with guns ready. They knew where the trouble was coming from. It was coming from the car, and they had it taped.

But this was nicer. The truck had its tires shot out from the side of the road, and an innocent little convertible coming on down the road held the boys who were going to put the guards down for the count. It was hardly an elaborate variation. For all McLeod knew, it had been tried before. But you didn't get anywhere with elaborate switches. It was the small tricks, the little twists, that made the difference. It was taking a good gambit and sharpening it so that it was perfect—that was what you had to do if you wanted to come out on top.

Burl finished. Everything was sharp, tight. It couldn't misfire. McLeod stood up.

"I'll see you," he said.

"Running, Marty?"

"Uh-huh."

"Got a babe waiting?"

"Sure," he said. "Ten of them."

He left. His Chevy was at the curb. He got into it and drove back to his shack, and she was waiting for him. He had known she would be there. They hadn't planned it, but he had started to feel her presence at the shack from the moment he had gotten into the Chevy outside of Burl's place. He could always tell with her. It was like telepathy. He could feel her, could know where she would be and what she would be doing.

When he walked in she was making coffee. The good

coffee smell filled the shack. She went to him and he kissed her. She put her arms around his waist, hugged him close.

"McLeod," she said.

He bent over, kissed her cheek, her throat. He tipped up her chin and kissed her mouth again, tasting the infinite sweetness of it. Her eyes were misty.

"Coffee's just about ready, McLeod."

"Pour me some."

The coffee was fresh and strong. It burned his mouth. He lit a cigarette, gave it to her. She took a drag and passed it back to him.

"How did it go?"

"Standard," he said.

"Was Jimmy there?"

He nodded.

"Poor Jimmy," she said.

"Why?"

"He wants me," she said. "And he can't have me. That's why he's poor Jimmy."

"Somehow," he told her, "I don't feel sorry for him."

"Neither do I."

"He's a punk."

"So are you, McLeod."

He laughed, picked her up effortlessly and cradled her in his arms. She fought a mock battle, then tossed her arms around his neck and kissed him. Just a little girl, he thought. Jailbait. A cockeyed mixture of young and old, hot as a firecracker and sweeter than maple syrup.

He kissed her again. She started to unbutton his shirt

and he didn't stop her. She pulled the shirt loose from his trousers and ran her hand over his naked chest. She tugged at a handful of chest hair and he groaned.

"Hurt you, McLeod?"

"Sure."

"Put me down, McLeod."

He let her down. He thought again about the problem that had bugged him at Burl's place. He could have twenty-five thousand dollars or the whole hundred grand. Which way was the right way? Which way?

"Finish your coffee, McLeod."

"Why?"

"Because I want you to make love to me."

"So?"

"So there's no sense wasting the coffee. It'll get cold if you don't finish it."

"Screw the coffee."

"Why screw the coffee," she said, "when you can screw me?"

Good question. He walked to the bedroom with her and took her clothes off, running his hands over her body. He dropped his pants, his underwear. He joined her on the bed and made love to her and the world went away.

For a time there was no job, no truck to be robbed, no money to be divided. For a time there was no town of Cedar Corners and no electric chair at McAllister and no tommy guns and nothing, nothing. There was no Burl, no Mike Lieber, no Jack Dawes, no Jimmy Kell.

There was only her.

Her—Betty Marie—sweet, warm, alive, beneath him, around him, moving, taking, receiving, loving...

Her.

And then, afterward, she heated more coffee and brought the cups into the bedroom. He sat drinking the coffee, sharing another cigarette with her. Twenty grand or a hundred grand? Part of it or all of it?

He knew the answer now.

All the way. Alone, there might have been another answer. Alone it might have been better to settle for a piece, a hunk. With her it was different. It had to be all the way. With her you could never settle for half.

He opened his mouth, then closed it. No need to tell her, no point in it. Tomorrow would be good enough for that. If they went for the whole bundle she would have to play a part, too. He knew she'd do whatever she had to do, knew she would kill if he told her to kill. But there was no reason to bother her with it just yet. There would be plenty of time for that later, the night before the job. It was Wednesday now, and the job was set for Friday, and that gave him another night to talk to her. Let her rest easy until then. She liked tension, she handled it the same way he did, but there was no reason to saddle her with extra troubles before it was necessary.

"McLeod—"

He turned to look at her.

"It's soon," she said.

"Day after tomorrow."

"What time will you get back from it?"

"Around noon, maybe earlier."

"And then?"

"Jimmy drives the car to Burl's," he said. "We stow the car in Burl's garage, with the money in it. We split up and lay low again. We meet around dinner time at Burl's and split the dough. Mike and Jack head for Rushville in time to make their planes out of here. You and I hop in the Chevy and get the hell away."

"In the Chevy?"

"Uh-huh. Pick up another car somewhere along the way. The Chevy won't be hot for a day or two, anyway."

She nodded, reached out a hand, ran it over his chest. She was breathing easily enough. A good kid, he thought. An amazing kid.

"McLeod—"

Her hand moved lower, over his chest, over his stomach. Her hand found him and held him.

"McLeod, don't get killed."

"I won't."

"Because I'd miss this," she said, squeezing it for emphasis. "I'd really miss this, McLeod."

Chapter 8

The hangover took seven hours to cure, which wasn't bad when you stopped to consider how long it had been building. Joyce had started hitting the bottle hard on Sunday, and when she awoke Monday she was still drunk, so she started in again before the edge had a chance to wear off. From that point on it was just round-the-clock drinking for Joyce Ramsdell.

Wednesday night was the last night of it. Thursday morning she didn't wake up drunk, because a siege of vomiting toward the end had knocked out some of the liquor that would have been in her bloodstream otherwise. In the morning she woke up suddenly, violently, and horribly.

She spent an hour puking, which was not particularly pleasant. Puking is rarely pleasant, but if you are drunk at the time you aren't nearly so aware of the degree of unpleasantness involved. When you are not only sober but also hungover, puking attains its highest degree of revoltingness.

It was revolting, all right.

But after an hour it was over. Then came the queasy feeling, and the coffee that didn't help very much, and the need for food but the nausea that the mere thought of food inspired, and all the rest.

Let's not go into it. If you have ever had a really top-drawer grade-A number-one hangover, you already know all about it, and a description would only awaken feelings of nostalgia in your bosom that might better be suppressed. And if you have never been damned with a hangover, such a description might well turn you off booze altogether, and that would be shameful. A man who avoids strong drink out of fear of the morning after is in a class with a man who avoids women on the chance that one of them might bear venereal tidings along with her love. As we all know, such men are rank fools.

But, at any rate, let us abandon describing Joyce Ramsdell's hangover. She had one. It was a rotten one. It lasted seven hours, or until four in the afternoon, and then, by God, it was mercifully over.

That's that.

When the hangover was gone, all the way gone, all that remained was a need.

She needed a man.

She got dressed and went out looking for one.

Burl's nerves were jumping. He was in his house, alone, and his nerves were on edge. Jack Dawes was upstairs with a paperback book. Everybody else was somewhere else. It was Thursday, and it was afternoon, and Burl was on edge.

That was what happened when you got down close to the wire, he thought. The job was hours away, an afternoon and a night, and then it was morning and they either won or they lost. He didn't see how they could lose, but you could always lose when you were playing for big stakes. Something could always go wrong. No matter how foolproof a job was, there was always something that could zoom in out of the blue and trip you up.

A trip now meant the end of the game, of the world.

He didn't want that to happen.

He jammed a cigar between his teeth on the left side of his mouth. He scratched a wooden match on the sole of one shoe, lit the cigar evenly. He puffed on it and expelled a cloud of smoke. He wanted a drink, but a drink now didn't make any sense. Before it had had a calming effect, but from here on in he wanted to be completely sober. The littlest dull spot could throw you off the track, ruin you completely.

So drinking was out.

He chewed the cigar. Maybe it made more sense to play it small, go on selling shine and handling small-town racket games and cooling it with what he had. It wasn't as though he was in a bind, for Christ's sake. He had a lot of things going for him and they brought the money in nice and steady. He could go on that way forever, paying off the people who had to be bought, dodging the others, and operating until he died with little fear of arrest and enough income to keep him very comfortable. You took a big chance when you played for one big score to put you on Easy Street. You chanced everything you had and more. You put it all up on the block, and if you missed it was all over but the burying.

But he had to take the chance.

How many chances did a man get? How many shots at the moon came to you in the course of a lifetime?

Not many.

And if you passed them up?

Then you were nowhere. Then you never really made it big, because you were too content to make it small. You had to make a grab for the brass ring every time it came close to you. If you had a clear shot at it, and if you could cut down the chances of missing the ring and falling off your horse, then you had to take the shot.

It was that simple.

But the nervousness didn't go away. How far was Newport? Too damn far, he thought. He couldn't drive down to Newport and have a party and come back. He'd be dead tired in the morning, and he wanted to be sharp as a razor. A trip to Newport would do it, though. A trip to Newport, a little session of watching two girls eat each other for lunch, that would do it. It always did. It eased the tension better than anything else in the world.

But Newport was out.

What else? Go around window-peeping? That never worked, not really. Burl was perverted and he knew it. He was a voyeur, and he got his kicks from watching, not from doing. He wasn't sure why he worked this way and he didn't really give a damn. That was the way it was.

It didn't have to be two girls. It could be a guy and a girl, something like that. But he liked to sit and watch until he relieved himself, and then he liked to go away.

That was all.

There was another way. He could sit, eyes closed, while a woman made oral love to him. He could do this, letting his mind wander, imagining things. But it was much better to sit alone and watch two other people. Infinitely better.

How?

He heard footsteps on the staircase. He jumped, then relaxed. It was Jack Dawes coming downstairs. The man lumbered heavily into the room, tossed his thick body into a chair.

"Jesus," he said.

"Something wrong?"

"You know it."

"What is it?"

"I need a woman," Jack said. "Now how in hell do you find a woman in a jerkwater town like this? I always need a woman before a job. There a cathouse here?"

Burl shook his head.

"There a cathouse anywhere *near* here?"

"No."

"Damn it to hell."

The thought came slowly. Burl drew on the cigar, took it from his mouth, focused on it. It was a good thought, all things considered. It might solve two people's problems. It just might work all across the board.

"I could find you a woman," he said slowly.

"Now?"

"Now."

"A pig?"

"A good looker," Burl said. "Good face, good figure. A tramp, but a good looker. And wild in bed."

Jack Dawes didn't say anything. He was watching Burl and his eyes were cagy.

"Interested?"

"First I want to hear the catch."

"What makes you think there's a catch?"

"There's gotta be."

Burl ducked ashes from the cigar. "There's a catch."

"Let's hear it."

"I watch," Burl said.

"Huh?"

"I watch. You do what you want with her—she'll do anything in the world and love it. You do whatever you want. But I watch, I sit there and I watch."

Dawes thought it over. Burl looked away, smoked. His hands were starting to tremble and he tried to control them with partial success. Go for it, he thought. Please, damn you, go for it. What do you care who watches? Go for it, have a ball, and I watch.

"That's your kick, Burl?"

"Yeah."

"I heard that," Dawes said. "You know, you hear a lot of things. That's the way you like it."

"That's the way I like it."

"The hell," Dawes said. "The hell, everybody has his own private kick. I won't complain."

"Then you go for it?"

"I want a woman," Dawes said. "You go and find her and bring her. Then watch all you want. Watch? Hell, you can take a roll of film. I don't give a damn. The way I feel I could bang a broad in Macy's window at high noon and not give a damn. Go find us a broad, Burl. Find a good one."

Burl nodded. He got to his feet, waddled out of the house. The broad had to be around, he thought. She had to be around and she had to be ready to go.

It figured that she would be.

Joyce Ramsdell was always ready to go.

Betty Marie looked up at the sky. It was getting dark. It was nice to ride in a convertible with the top down, nice to be able to lean back and look at the sky. It was a shame, in a way, that McLeod didn't own a convertible. Well, maybe they would get one sooner or later. They'd probably run through a lot of cars before they hit Mexico, or the coast, or wherever in hell they were going. She didn't care what they rode in, she decided. Just so they didn't take the last ride in a hearse.

"Betty Marie—"

"What?"

Jimmy turned to face her. "Listen," he said. "Listen," he said. "Listen, it's tomorrow. You got that?"

"I know."

"In the morning, early."

"Well?"

She knew what he meant, but it would be fun to make him fight to get the words out.

"Well what?"

He took a deep breath. He was driving slowly now, one hand on the wheel, his other arm around her. She hated to have him touch her—she wanted to be touched by McLeod and nobody else. But at the same time it was a kick to tease him, to make him think he was her man while all the while she was sleeping with McLeod.

"I could be dead tomorrow," he said.

"I know, Jimmy."

"I could be dead. If we . . . if we made love tonight, at least I'd die happy."

She couldn't have thought up a cornier line if she had had three years to work on it. It was hard not to laugh, but she gritted her teeth and managed it. He'd die happy? That was one for the books, all right.

"We can't," she said.

"But—"

"I've still got my period, Jimmy."

"So?"

"Don't be disgusting."

"Maybe we could—"

"You don't understand at all," she said. "I couldn't enjoy anything during my period. I don't have any feeling for sex then. I don't even like it when you put your arm around me."

He didn't take the hint, instead edged his hand closer to

her breast. Go ahead, she thought. The feel you cop may be your last, Jimmy Boy.

"Betty Marie—"

He said her name, then gave up. He drove around a while longer, trying to convince her that she would be doing immeasurable service to God and to her country if she were only willing to part either her thighs or her lips to accommodate him, but her answer remained the same. Finally she decided to toss him a bone. There was a certain amount of poetic beauty in it.

"Jimmy," she said, "I'll be done tomorrow."

"Tomorrow?"

"That's right. When you come back from ... from the job, I'll be at the quarry. Just come straight to the quarry and I'll be there."

"Baby—"

"And we'll do whatever you want," she said. "I'll really want you then. I'll be burning up for you, after a week of having to go without it. And you'll be through with the job, and you'll be all proud and happy, and it'll be a ball."

It would be a ball, all right. It would be beautiful. He would go to the quarry like a trusting puppy, all hot and bothered, and she wouldn't be there. And the next thing he knew she would be out of town with McLeod, out of his life forever.

It would be a ball.

*   *   *

Burl found her at the Corners Tavern. She was standing at the bar between a pair of drunks and she was working on a slug of bourbon. She didn't look drunk. He guessed that it was her first drink of the evening.

"Well, now," he said. "Hello, Joyce."

She gave him a smile.

"I got a fellow over to my place," he said. "Real nice fellow. He was telling me he'd like to meet a girl."

"I'm not a hooker," she said.

One of the drunks stared at her, then looked away. The barman found something to do at the other end of the bar. Burl grinned at her, let the grin die slowly.

"I know that," he said.

"So—"

"My friend don't want a hooker," he went on. "Wants a nice girl, like yourself. This is a real friend of mine, Joyce. A fine fellow. I think the two of you ought to get along fine. I think you'll take a shine to each other."

He watched her face. It gave her away; he could tell that she wanted it, that she was dying for it. And he knew enough to guess she wouldn't care if he watched. She'd probably like it better that way, from what he knew about her. She liked a little extra thrill to make things more exciting. She was that kind of a woman.

"You aren't a pimp, are you?"

"Not me, Joyce. I'm helping out a friend."

"That's all?"

"A friend of mine from out of town," he said. "I'm doing

him a good turn. Of course, you might say that I have an interest in it myself."

"What?"

He looked at her. God, what a pair of boobs! It would be nice to watch Jack get to her. The two of them ought to put on one hell of a show.

"I want to watch," he said.

It took a few minutes, but no more than that. At first she told him he was some kind of a nut, and then she told him he must be kidding, and next she asked him what kind of a girl he thought she was. He let that one go unanswered, and next thing he knew she decided it would be interesting, and something she'd never done before. He bought her another drink and had one for himself, and then he took her fleshy arm and led her out of the tavern and over to his car. He hurried her home, trembling now, excited now, ready now for the special kick that would ease his tension once and for all.

He opened the door, led her inside. Jack looked up, saw, and was pleased. She looked at Jack and was just as pleased. And Burl was happy.

"I'll go now," he told them, after showing them through to the bedroom. "I'll give you two a chance to get to know each other a little better. You have fun now, you hear?"

"Sure," Jack said.

"Don't stay away too long," Joyce said.

Burl went out, walked down the hallway to the living room. He started to unwrap a cigar, then changed his mind and took a cigarette instead. A cigar would take too long.

He didn't want to be away from the bedroom for that much time. A cigarette was more like it.

He listened, trying to hear sounds from the bedroom. He couldn't hear anything. Right now they would be kissing, he thought. Then they'd be getting undressed. Then he would be touching her, handling her breasts—

Burl was happy. In the morning the job would go like clockwork, and he'd be richer by a fortune, and in the meantime he had a floorshow to watch.

Well, now, he thought. Well, now.

Betty Marie got away from Jimmy a few minutes after she made the date to meet him at the quarry around noon. She left him, and started walking to McLeod's shack. McLeod would be there, waiting for her. And she wanted to see him.

He wasn't there. The shack was empty, and she stood for a moment wondering where he had gone. His car was there but McLeod wasn't. Then she heard the gunshots and she knew where to find him. He was in the fields practicing with the pistol. She went to him slowly, watching him aim quickly, squeeze off a shot, and send the bullet to the mark.

It gave her a thrill to watch. McLeod was good with the gun, almost perfect. And there was something tremendously sexual about watching him shoot the gun. The symbolism wasn't enormously subtle. The gun was a mechanical phallus and McLeod was screwing the target to death.

"Hi," she said.

He turned sharply, gun in hand, then relaxed when he saw it was her. "I got tired of waiting," he said. "I wanted to sharpen up a little. Come on—let's get back to the shack."

"Keep on shooting, if you want."

"Forget it. Let's go."

They walked back arm in arm. With the fingers of one hand she touched the gun, ran her fingertips over the smooth metal hide of the thing. Nice, she thought. And in the morning McLeod would kill people with the gun. Very nice.

In the shack he put the gun away, then found two cans of beer in the refrigerator and opened them. He gave one to her, kept the other for himself. She took a long swig of the beer and grinned across the room at him.

"I thought you weren't drinking," she said.

"A beer won't hurt. And it's a hot night."

"I'm kidding."

"I know," he said. He didn't say anything for a few minutes and she remained silent, waiting. He had something to say to her. She could tell.

Finally he said: "Suppose you had your choice between twenty-five thousand dollars and a hundred thousand. Which would you take, kitten?"

"That's easy."

"Is it?"

"Sure," she said.

"Which?"

"The hundred thousand. I don't understand, McLeod."

He took her hand, drew small circles with his index

finger on the back of it. She looked at his eyes. She had an idea what he was talking about, a vague and half-formed idea, but she wanted to hear him say it.

"There's a hundred thousand dollars in this job," he said. "And I can't think of a decent reason why we shouldn't have every last cent of it."

She didn't speak.

"There are four other guys to split with, kitten. If something happened to them, there wouldn't be any split required."

"If they got killed?"

"Something like that."

She didn't have to hesitate. She didn't even have to think about it. She looked at him, her face completely serious. She said: "It's fine with me, McLeod."

"Is it?"

"Of course. We're dead anyway, if they catch us. And you might as well hang for a sheep as a lamb. And with the others dead we have a better chance to get away. Nobody'll be able to talk and nobody'll know who to look for. We can run faster once the rest of them are dead."

It was funny, being able to talk so coolly about death. But she was cool as ice now. She and McLeod had each other, and they were on a motorboat ride to hell, and she was happy. There was nothing to sweat about. Everything was fine.

"The job'll go the way it was supposed to," he said. "Except it'll play differently afterward. Burl has Jack Dawes staying over at his house. Lieber has a room in a rooming house. I'll get Lieber first. I'll walk him home and kill him in his room. He won't even know what's happening."

"Then?"

"Then I'll get Burl and Dawes. They won't be any trouble. They'll think I'm coming over for my split. I'll get them both and pick up the dough. All of it."

"You forgot somebody, McLeod."

"Jimmy?"

"Jimmy."

"I didn't forget him," he said. "I thought he could have an accident during the job. He could catch a stray bullet."

"Then who drives?"

"I can drive."

"He's a better driver, McLeod. And it doesn't make any sense. Leave Jimmy for me."

"Are you crazy?"

"He's meeting me afterward," she said. "He's meeting me at the quarry. The asshole thinks I'm finishing my period in the morning and he can't wait to get his dick in me. I'll take care of him then, McLeod."

He was staring at her.

"Please," she said. "I'm not kidding."

"I know you're not."

"I can do it."

"Are you sure?"

"I'm positive."

"You're only a girl—"

"So?" She laughed. "He's not going to worry about me

killing him. He'll be all ready to make love. He'll be dead without knowing it, McLeod."

She talked him into it. It would be beautiful, perfect. She would get him with a knife, a nice small knife that would slip into his back and reach for his heart. Then he would twitch and moan, and then he would be dead.

Perfect.

"We'll do it that way," he said finally. "Just roll him into the water and he'll be out of the way for a long time. Then you stay there. I'll pick you up at the quarry as soon as I get finished with everything else."

"You know where it is?"

"I know where it is."

"All right," she said. "I'll take good care of Jimmy Kell. And then I'll wait for you."

"It won't bother you, will it? Waiting there?"

"Not me, McLeod."

"You're icy cool," he said, admiringly.

"That's not true."

"It isn't?"

She moved closer to him, let him feel the swell of her taut young breasts against the side of his arm.

"Not icy," she said.

"I guess not."

"Not even cool," she said. "Talking about it is making me all hot and bothered, McLeod."

"That's good."

"Is it?"

"Uh-huh," he said. "Because I'm going to take you to bed now, kitten. Come on."

She went with him and her whole body was shaking like a leaf. God, she thought. God in heaven, what a sleigh ride we're on. In the morning they would rob the truck, and then he would kill three men while she killed one, and then they'd run like rabbits with a hundred thousand beautiful dollars in their kick.

But first they would make love.

They were naked by the time Burl opened the door and slipped into the bedroom. They were naked, and they were on the bed, and he knew right away that it was going to be good. Good? It would be better than good. It would be perfect.

He found a chair, eased himself down onto it. He did not make any noise. He sat down, and he took a very deep breath, and he watched.

Joyce was on her back, her hair spread out over the pillow. Her eyes were wide open. She was breathing heavily, her chest heaving, her big breasts bobbing crazily.

Dawes was at her side. He was visibly excited, and his hands were busy with her body. Burl watched him touch her thighs, pat her stomach, reach for her huge breasts.

Dawes squeezed. Dawes poked the mounds of flesh, probed them. Dawes handled her bluntly but expertly, and she began to writhe on the bed, and Burl's eyes stared at the two of them. Good, he thought. Just fine.

Joyce reached for him, hauled him down to her. Joyce was bouncing all over the bed, her whole body churning like butter in a tub.

Well, now!

Burl watched, his eyes bulging. He watched when Dawes straightened up, knelt over her, then began to swing his hand back and forth, slapping her across the breasts. Joyce didn't seem to mind. Her breasts quivered, accepting the punishment, drawing pleasure from it. Dawes slapped her back and forth, slapped her nipples till they tingled. Dawes leaned over slightly, wrapping each of his big hands around a breast. He leaned back, pulling her up, then flipped her over onto her stomach.

He dropped her, let her lie face down. He began slapping again, giving her buttocks a workout, slapping them until they were flaming red. Burl had never seen anything like this. It was good watching a pair of whores have fun with each other, but this cut it sixteen ways. This was tough, strong, vital. This had guts.

Slap!

Slap!

Slap!

Then Dawes had a hand on either side of her, gripping, lifting. He drew Joyce to a kneeling position, held her that way.

Burl stared.

And Dawes was taking her.

God!

Burl was watching, wide-eyed. He saw Joyce moving and heaving, saw Joyce sweating and straining. And he saw Dawes riding like a cowboy on a bucking bronco, riding like a champion, punishing her and pleasuring her at once.

It was the beginning of the world and the end of the world. It was the whole world, slashing down a ski slope, diving into the deep end of the pool of Hell. It was wild and wonderful, vicious and vile, depraved and delicious.

And Burl watched it all.

Chapter 9

A great many things happened on Friday.

There was a revolt in a Latin American country, for example. The revolt was crushed in three hours by troops loyal to the government, and fifty perpetrators of the rebellion were publicly flayed alive and their skins hung from the walls of the governmental palace.

There was a bomb test in the Soviet Union which provoked a protest from the American ambassador to the United Nations, and there was a bomb test in Nevada which provoked a protest from the Russian ambassador to the United Nations. There was a cholera epidemic in Tibet, an earthquake of sorts in San Francisco, and the Dow Jones industrial average was up significantly.

Now all of these phenomena, while no doubt of interest to some souls, are hardly important to us here and now. We've been concerning ourselves with the activities of a group of persons in the town of Cedar Corners. And, you may be happy to note, a great many things happened there.

All on Friday.

*   *   *

The first significant event took place in a house on Walnut Street at three in the morning. Sandra Craig was alone in her house at the time. Luke Penner had left a few hours ago, and Sandra was alone, and it happened.

She sat for a long time in front of the mirror on her dressing table. She sat looking at her reflection. She could see her face, which was pretty, and her breasts, which were large. She looked at her face, and at her breasts, and she decided that she hated herself with a passion.

For two years she had been a widow. Admittedly, she had not been the happiest widow in creation. She would remember Rudy Craig, and she would remember how she had loved him, and she would be unhappy. But at least she had managed to live a regular life, a sane and sensible life. Sometimes she was lonely, and sometimes she felt the need for a man, but in the main she had been living a relatively happy life.

Until Luke Penner came along.

Then everything had gone wrong, somehow. He had come to her, unwanted and uninvited, and he had made love to her. She didn't want him to make love to her the first time. She never wanted him. She wished, each time, that she would never have to see him again.

Each time, like a bad penny or a bad Penner, he came back. Each time, no matter how much she fought with him, she would end up wanting him. Each time he made love to her, and each time she enjoyed it, needed it, ached for it. No matter how much she hated him—and she hated him a little more each time—she still loved it when they made love.

Not from the start. At first she would hate that, too, but as he worked on her the hate turned to lust and she was caught up in a web of passion.

And she wound up enjoying it. And he left, and she hated him more than ever, and hated herself more than ever, and it went on and on and on.

There was only one way out.

At 3:15 in the morning, on Friday, Sandra Craig took that only way out.

She started with a razor blade. She held the blade in one hand and slashed her breasts. She was cutting in front of her mirror at the time, and she watched her mirror image as she sliced first the left and then the right breast with the blade. Thin lines of red blood appeared on each breast. There was probably some pain involved, but Sandra Craig did not feel it. She was in a state of shock. She felt nothing.

She cut again, again. She lacerated her nipples until they dropped beads of blood on the dressing table before her. Then she went to slash her wrists, and she made marks on one wrist without getting the vein and then she realized that it would never work that way. It is surprisingly difficult to slash your wrists and kill yourself. The body fights to live. There had to be an easier way.

There was.

She found a length of strong clothesline in the kitchen, looped it over an exposed beam in the living room. She pulled a chair over under the beam, stepped upon the chair, made a slip knot in one end of the rope, anchored the other end, and fitted the noose over her head and around her neck. She tightened the noose until it was tight around her throat, then adjusted the rope so that it ran taut from the beam to her neck.

Then she kicked the chair out of the way.

When public executioners do it, it works differently. There's a fall, and there's a hangman's noose positioned so that the neck breaks, and death comes rather quickly. But she was hanging herself with a clothesline instead of a heavier rope, and she wasn't using the proper knot and she didn't have enough of a drop.

Death didn't come quickly at all.

It came slowly.

She hung there, choking, her bare legs flailing ineffectually at empty air. Blood was dripping freely from both breasts now. She tried to reach the floor with her feet and failed. She tried to grip the rope above her head so that she could ease the pressure on her throat, but she couldn't do that either. She would manage for a moment, but then her body weight would be too much for her to support and she would lose her grip on the rope. The pain was horrible, and it went on forever, and she wished that she had chosen a better way to kill herself, and then she began to wish that she had merely decided to stay alive, and then she wished she had never been born in the first place.

She died, finally.

It took her a little over an hour.

*   *   *

At four-thirty, Jimmy Kell got out of bed. He couldn't sleep. He was excited about everything at once, and sleep was no longer possible, and he wanted to start getting ready. He took a quick shower, went down to the Land's End for a quick breakfast, and stood outside in the cool air of early morning smoking cigarettes and waiting for it to be time to get the show on the road. He was supposed to drive over to Burl's. They were all going to meet there, and then they would get started.

They were going to have a gun for him, but he didn't figure he would have to use it. He hoped not. He didn't know much about guns, had hardly fired one, and had never even had a pistol in his hand. There were four of them; they ought to be able to handle the shooting without him. Of course, it would be good to have a gun just in case. And he could try a few shots even if he didn't hit anybody.

The guards would be shooting at him.

It was as though he was realizing this precious fact for the first time. Whether he had a gun or not, the guards would be trying to kill him. They would come out of the truck spraying lead, and the lead would be headed in his direction, and they would be trying to kill him.

Suppose he got shot.

Oh, Jesus. Jesus, you could go nuts that way. He had to believe that everything would turn out all right. Otherwise he would get cold feet and chicken blood and he'd be in trouble. He couldn't back out, not now. They needed him. And if he tried to chicken out they would kill him. He had to stay with it, even if he didn't want to.

Didn't want to? Hell, he wanted to. Five grand was plenty of dough to get just for driving a car. Five grand was a lot of money. And there was more to it—he'd have an in with the right boys, he'd have a strong reputation that would make things a lot easier for him.

He wanted it, didn't he?

The hell with it, he told himself. It didn't make a damn bit of difference what he wanted.

He was stuck with it.

McLeod got out of bed a few minutes after five. Betty Marie had left around midnight—he'd made her go, told her he needed a good night's sleep. And, amazingly, he had slept. A hot shower, a glass of ice water, and he had slept like a log.

He had set the clock, but now he turned it off before it could ring. He had a clock inside his head, and that had taken care of getting him out of bed on time. He washed up, dressed, made a cup of coffee. He loaded the gun with a full magazine and stuck it under the waistband of his slacks. He filled an envelope with extra shells and stuck it into a pocket.

He left the shack, stood for a moment in the front yard. If he drove over to Burl's house, he could give Mike Lieber a ride back, go upstairs with him, kill him, and then drive back to Burl's. If he walked, he'd walk back with Lieber, then walk back to Burl's. It might be tricky with the car, but it was better to have it with him all the time. He opened a door, got behind the wheel, and drove over to Burl's place.

The clock woke Burl. He got up, rubbing at his eyes with clenched fists. He was on a couch in the living room. Dawes and Joyce were in his bed. He had left them there when he went to sleep.

For all he knew, they were still going at it.

The door to the bedroom was open. He walked over there. They were both asleep, sprawled out cold on the big bed. He walked over to Dawes, shook him by the shoulder.

"Jack," he said.

No response.

He shook him again, harder. "Jack—"

Dawes opened one eye, blinked it, opened the other eye. "Jesus Christ," he said.

"It's time."

"Already?"

"Already."

"Jesus Christ."

Burl sighed. "Come on," he said. "Get up and get dressed. I'll get some coffee started."

"What about the broad?"

He looked at Joyce. She hadn't moved a muscle since he walked into the room.

"Let her sleep," be said. "You didn't tell her anything about the job, did you?"

"I didn't even tell her my name."

"Good. Then let her sleep."

"She's some broad, man."

"I know," Burl said.

Dawes chuckled. "Yeah," he said. "I guess you know that, don't you? I mean, you saw whatever there was to see."

Burl turned, left the room. He put up a pot of coffee. It was ready by the time Dawes came out of the room. He poured coffee for both of them and they sat down and sipped it.

"I oughta leave the broad a note," Dawes said.

"Why?"

"So she'll be here when we get back. I'm going to want her when we get back."

"She'll be here."

"Yeah?"

"She won't go away. Not if she figures she can get more of what she got last night."

"She can get all she wants," Dawes said. "All she god-damn well wants, she can get."

They were halfway through with the coffee when Jimmy Kell drove up, all the way done when Mike Lieber arrived. McLeod came a few minutes after him. They sat around, talking in monosyllables, and then it was time.

They filed out of the house and got into the Pontiac convertible. Jimmy Kell settled in behind the wheel. Jack Dawes sat next to him and Mike Lieber had the window seat, so that he could get out in a hurry. Burl and McLeod were in the back.

"Put the top up," Burl said.

Jimmy put the top up. It was good weather for driving with the top down, but that would have been stupid.

"Go," Burl said.

Jimmy turned the key in the ignition, stepped on the gas. He didn't leave a patch of rubber on the pavement this time. He drove steadily and quietly out of town and headed northeast on Route 147.

The armored truck left Indianapolis right on schedule. There was the driver and a guard in front, three guards in the back with the money. The driver was named Roy Cole, and the man beside him was named Jeff Carr. The three guards in the back were named Dan Moyer, Lou Gangler, and Ed Hunt. These names are not especially important, and may be forgotten at will. The important thing is that the armored truck left Indianapolis on schedule and made good time on the way.

The truck stopped on schedule at Paulling, pulling up in front of the Paulling truck company. There were five bank guards on hand, plus a vice-president who was in charge of the transfer of funds from truck to vault. Roy Cole, the driver, pressed a button to signal the boys in the back that everything was all right. He got out on his side of the truck, and Jeff Carr got out his side. They walked around to the back. Moyer, Gangler and Hunt came out with their guns ready. They helped the bank guards lug a sack of money into the bank, saw that it was locked in the vault, and got back into the truck again.

They were still right on schedule. The next stop was Centreville, just a few miles farther on 147.

Betty Marie slept late, as late as she could. She woke up hungry and dazed. She went downstairs, had breakfast, and got out of the house before anybody could start a conversation with her. McLeod was busy with the job now and she was nervous.

She took a knife with her when she left the house, an ordinary kitchen knife with a five-inch blade and a black wooden handle. It was just the right sort of knife to use on Jimmy Kell, long enough to reach his heart, small enough so that it wouldn't be too bulky.

The sun was hot, high in the sky already. She put the knife in her pocket and walked along the edge of town and then toward the quarry. It was early now—too early for the job to be over, but she stood nothing to gain by waiting. She could be at the quarry early, and she could plan everything out, and when Jimmy arrived it would all go smoothly.

She smiled.

It was a long walk to the quarry. She smoked a few cigarettes on the way there, and she stopped from time to time to take the knife from the pocket of her dungarees and examine it, checking to make sure it felt right in her hand, feeling the weight of it and gauging the balance of it.

Soon, she thought.

Soon.

She kept walking, rehearsing it in her mind. Jimmy would come to her, flushed with triumph, feeling like the biggest man in the world. He would come to her, aching for her, and she would meet him neatly and perfectly, would use that knife to reach his heart and stop it from beating forever.

I'm going to kill somebody, she thought.

Kill. Murder. It seemed impossible, but then everything seemed impossible. Not long ago she had been a virgin, destined to marry Luke Penner and spend the rest of her life in Cedar Corners. Now she was a gun moll, for God's sake. She was a robber's woman, and she was going to be a murderess in her own right.

And she seemed to take to it well enough. Bad blood? A vicious streak? She had no idea what it was, and she did not much give a damn. Whatever it was, it was there. Whatever she was, she was going to do her part well.

She kept on walking until she reached the quarry. Then she sat down, tense but happy, and waited.

Sandra Craig's door was not locked. This surprised Luke; generally he had to ring the bell until she answered it, but now it was closed and not locked. Well, maybe she only locked it at night. He had never come to see her in the morning before, but it was morning now and he had nothing to do and he wanted her again, so here he was.

He stood for a moment or two in front of the door,

waiting. Fun, he thought. What would he do with teach today? Something cute, he decided. Something new. Not beat her—that was fun, but it had its limitations. It would be better to make her do something she didn't want to do. Something filthy, something perverted, something that would make the bitch vomit.

He thought of something.

Then he opened the door. But it evidently wasn't the day for him to make Sandra Craig vomit. Quite the reverse happened, as it turned out.

She made *him* vomit.

She was hanging by the neck and she was dead. Her neck had stretched to an impossible length, and her face was swollen and purple with death, her hands and feet a dark blue. There were blood stains on her breasts, and there were puddles of blood on the floor where her breasts had dripped redness. She was dead and she was horrible in death, and he threw up seconds after he caught sight of her. His stomach turned over completely and he heaved up his breakfast all over the floor.

He was sick for a long time. He couldn't look at her without being sick, so he left the house, being careful to lock the door on the way out.

She was dead.

And he had killed her.

It was suicide, of course. But she would never have committed suicide if it hadn't been for him. He had driven her to it. He had pushed her and injured her, and he had been the instrument in her death.

The sin was on his head.

He walked, dazed, to his car. What was going to happen to him? For God's sake, what *had* happened to him? He'd been a quiet kid, the quietest of kids, a kid who had his mother worried because he was picking out such a potentially dull life for himself.

Dull? Not any more. First he went to a prostitute in Rushville. Then he learned about lust from a woman named Joyce Ramsdell. Then he pushed over a few pushovers, and finally he taught a young widow the meaning of sin, and now that widow was dead by her own hand and it was all his fault.

It had been so simple before, so simple and so easy. He was going to marry Betty Marie James. He was going to pump gas at his father's Texaco station. He was going to—

He was going to be in trouble.

They would find her. They would know it was his fault, they would make the connection somehow, and he would be washed up as far as the town of Cedar Corners was concerned. His mother would hate him and his father would hate him and the whole town would hate him.

He was in trouble.

He got into his car, started the engine. He hardly knew what he was doing, knew only that he had to get the hell out of Cedar Corners in a hurry. He was in trouble, in trouble, in trouble. He had to rush, had to hurry, had to get out of town.

Suppose they thought he killed her? He couldn't prove

otherwise. Maybe they would try to get him for murder. Maybe—

He took 147 out of town, heading in the general direction of Indianapolis. He drove as fast as he could and the car ate up miles of highway.

Jimmy drove beautifully. He wasn't trying to push the car, was only trying to stay as close to schedule as he possibly could. The traffic was light on 147, almost nonexistent. He held the car at a steady five miles an hour above the speed limit, losing no time behind trucks and no time on curves. He drove like a machine and the Pontiac convertible did everything it was supposed to do. They stayed right on schedule, moving along in perfect order.

Dawes was next to him. Dawes wasn't thinking about the job now. Dawes wasn't the type of guy who did a lot of thinking. When a job came along, he functioned more like a robot than like a human being. He was a supremely efficient robot and he did everything he was supposed to do just as he was supposed to do it, but he didn't have to think about it.

Instead, he was thinking about Joyce. She had given him a workout last night, and she had taken everything he had dished out, and she had loved every minute of it. A tramp, a lousy tramp, but nice. Nice to have waiting for him when he got back. Nice to round out the morning with. Then he'd leave her and take his twenty grand and get the hell away. You could do a lot with twenty grand. You could find a lot of willing broads.

Mike Lieber was sitting next to Dawes. The chopper was still in the guitar case and the case was across his lap. Mike was not thinking of the job either, but that was not because he didn't think while he worked. He generally did a great deal of thinking, and he had already done a tremendous amount of thinking about this particular job. He was not thinking now because there was no reason to do so. Everything would go according to plan. It was a simple plan and it would be easy.

He was thinking instead about his wife and two daughters. He lived in a suburb of Chicago and he was happily married. His wife had no idea how he made a living. She thought he did something in the stock market, but she was not sure what it was.

Once or twice or three times a year Mike accepted a job. He never got caught. If the job turned sour, he got out of it. If it stayed sweet he collected. He'd never been arrested and he did not intend to be arrested. He was a professional criminal contractor, a man who lived a double life and brought it off perfectly and he was thinking about his wife and daughters and how good it would be to get home to them.

Burl's mind was on money. He sat in back with the second submachinegun across his knees and thought about money. He had told them there would be a hundred grand in the job. With a little luck, the take should be double that amount. Instead of thirty grand—a proper cut, since he had set everything up and since he had handled the cash outlay—instead of that, he would be getting something like a hundred and thirty grand, if the truck was toting a decent load. Burl sat there thinking about money, waiting for it to come to him.

McLeod was thinking about everything. He was thinking about the job, about his chances of coming out of it on top. His chances look good. He had been trying to decide if anyone else was planning the same sort of surprise he had on tap, and he didn't think anyone was setting him up. Dawes didn't have the brains for a double-cross and the kid who was driving didn't have the guts. Burl wasn't the double-cross type, and Lieber looked too much like a competent workman who would never dream of making an executive decision.

So he was the only one looking to get everything for himself. Good. The job itself would be easy enough. What about the second job? What about the double-cross?

It was easier the fewer men had to be killed back in town. If he could leave one corpse on the road, he was that much ahead. Not Jimmy, because the kid could drive like hell, all in all, and because Betty Marie was going to take care of him anyway. And not Burl, certainly, because he was the center of everything. Leave him on the road and everyone would want to split on the spot.

That left Lieber and Dawes. If Lieber got it, that would make one less trip in town. But Lieber would be a tough man to hit. His post was across on the other side of the road. It would be handy to have him there, too, to keep the armored truck in a crossfire.

Dawes? That made more sense. Otherwise, with both Dawes and Burl at Burl's house, he'd have to get two of them at once. It was a longshot, taking out two men without tipping off the rest of the players. And he liked a game more when the odds were more on his side. Burl alone would be a cinch. Burl and Dawes might be tougher.

McLeod looked at his watch. It was getting close now, damned close. He pulled his gun out from the waistband of his slacks and ran his hands over the metal. His body heat had warmed it. He was good with the gun, was damned good with the gun. But he had never fired it at a person before. Maybe it was different with a living target.

He'd tried birds and squirrels, and it was no harder to pull the trigger, but they were small and they moved, and made elusive targets.

People were larger, easier to fix in your sights. But it might be harder to pull the trigger. And it didn't exactly simplify things when the human target was shooting back.

Forget it, he told himself. *Just fucking forget it.* Nobody was counting on him to gun down any of the guards. The choppers were designed to do most of the work. He was mainly there for mop-up operations, on the chance that he might get lucky and nail a guard with a lucky well-placed shot.

He wanted a cigarette, decided to pass it up. His hand was sweating. He switched the gun to his left hand, wiped his right hand dry on his pants leg, switched hands again.

Burl said: "Drop Mike right about here."

The convertible slowed, stopped. Mike Lieber opened the guitar case and took out the chopper. He left the case in the car and dogtrotted across the road with the chopper under one arm. He dropped down at the side of the road and got ready.

"Turn around."

Jimmy nodded. He dropped the Pontiac down into first, took a neat U-turn.

"About two hundred yards, kid."

Jimmy drove back about two hundred yards. Burl thought it over and told him to double the yardage. The kid drove along further, spun around in another U and stopped at the side of the road.

"Now we wait," Burl said.

Dawes was moving over toward the window, giving Jimmy room and making room for himself. He had his own gun out. Burl rolled down his window, steadied the muzzle of the chopper on the door-frame. He and Jimmy would be staying with the car; McLeod and Dawes would leave it and spread out.

A car went by, fast. *Damn you,* McLeod thought. *Just hurry up, bastard. Just don't be in the middle when the fun starts.* A goddamn trick like that could gum things up.

The car covered the four hundred yards and passed Lieber. McLeod and Burl let their breath out simultaneously, and Dawes said something about God.

McLeod reached for a cigarette again, stopped himself. Soon, he thought. Soon, and it better be right, it better work, it better be good. Suppose Lieber missed the tires? Hell, could you miss with a chopper? You could. The truck would be doing forty-five or fifty when it passed Lieber. You can miss a lot of things at that speed unless you're very goddamn good. Lieber was supposed to be very goddamn good and McLeod hoped to hell he was.

Jimmy had the clutch in. He was feeding gas to the motor, letting it growl. He wanted to be off like a shot the minute Lieber opened up with the chopper. This time, dammit, there would be one hell of a patch on the pavement. Gravel was going to fly.

They waited.

A fly hovered, settled on McLeod's nose. He brushed it away. The fly buzzed around and came back. He brushed it away again and cursed quietly.

Then it happened. Lieber's gun chattered like an angry magpie and Jimmy popped the clutch and the Pontiac roared forward, ready for the game.

They were into it now, win or lose.

Chapter 10

At that particular moment, Luke Penner was barreling down 147, the accelerator pedal on the floor and the wind singing in his ears.

At that particular moment, Sandra Craig's body, so nude and so dead, was swaying softly in her living room.

At that particular moment, Betty Marie James was sitting near the water's edge at the quarry, running her thumb across the blade of the knife.

At that particular moment, Mike Lieber sprayed the wheels of the heavy truck with a shower of hot lead. If you know how to use a submachine gun, know how to control it and keep it from riding up on you, you do not have to be particularly good to hit a target, moving or not. As with a shotgun, you don't aim the thing. All you do is point it.

Mike knew how to use a chopper. He got three of the truck's tires and blew them to hell and gone. The truck went into a spin, careening like a drunk on a rowboat in choppy waters. First it plunged toward the side of the road.

Then it swerved and headed across the road, then dipped, then shuddered.

When the tires went, Roy Cole was tossed against the steering wheel, then knocked back violently. He split his lip and lost two teeth in the front of his upper jaw. He did not lose consciousness. He had a gun in his hand and he was opening the door of the cab. The truck had not rolled. The door opened with no trouble.

Jack Carr, who had been sitting beside the driver in the cab of the truck, would normally have gone through the windshield. He was wearing a seat belt, however, and he stayed in place. He got out his gun and readied himself for a battle.

In the back of the truck, with the money, the three guards were knocked around for a few moments. One of them crashed into the side of the truck and broke an arm. The other two piled up in a corner, with neither one suffering any serious damage. They got up, flipped the rear doors open, and spilled out of the truck with their submachine guns going.

Then the convertible came up in front.

McLeod wasn't tense now. He felt nothing, nothing at all. He had been transformed from man to machine and the transformation was complete. He functioned without thinking, without feeling. He steadied himself when Jimmy slammed on the Pontiac's brakes, then threw open the door on his side and hit the dirt. He crawled on all fours, scurrying around to the rear of the convertible. He took his position, looked at the truck.

The driver had the door open and was on his way out. He evidently figured that the trouble was in the rear, where Mike Lieber had been. He didn't think of the Pontiac right off the bat, and Jack Dawes didn't give him time to think. Dawes shot him with his pistol, pumped a pair of slugs into Roy Cole's chest. He fell like a stone and didn't move. A fountain of blood burst from the twin holes in his chest.

McLeod cursed. The other one in the front seat had been on his way around the front of the truck before he heard Dawes' shot, but the shot stopped him and he was playing it cagy now, holding his cover behind the truck.

Burl was crouching in the back seat of the convertible, his chopper spitting a steady stream at the rear of the truck. McLeod crouched again, scurried to his left a few yards. It would work best with a cut-off, he thought. If he could come in at an angle, the guards would have no place to hide. And if Lieber could put on some pressure from the rear—

The chopper's chatter came in answer to the thought. Lieber was on the side of the road, running toward the truck and firing at the same time. The diversion worked. Lieber didn't hit anybody, but he drew enough attention for McLeod to cut across the road. He drew a bead with the .38, snapped off two quick shots at the guard who had been sitting next to the driver. The first one was wide. The second took the guard in the shoulder, spilling him. McLeod ran at him. The guard got off one shot and the bullet plowed up the gravel at McLeod's feet.

Then McLeod shot him. He put one slug in the side of Jeff Carr's face and watched him die.

One, he thought insanely. One man I killed. The first. How many more?

Just one more, as it turned out. There were three guards remaining. Burl got two of them with a burst from the chopper, taking them low and cutting their legs out from under them. Jack Dawes finished the pair, giving them each a coup de grace in the head. And Mike Lieber cut the last one to ribbons just as he was spraying bullets at Dawes.

The guard missed Dawes. But McLeod didn't miss. McLeod aimed the .38, squeezed the trigger. The shot wasn't perfect. It got Dawes in the chest but missed the heart. He fell, bleeding badly, and he was lying still when Lieber finished the last guard.

Then McLeod ran across the road to join the party.

It happened too quickly for Luke.

First he was just driving, paying no attention because you didn't have to pay much attention to a dull patch of road you'd driven hundreds of times. Then suddenly out of nowhere there was a truck in the road, standing almost in his path, and then there was a convertible parked in front of him motionless, and there wasn't enough space between the two of them for him to get through. He thought suddenly that he was going to crash, and then he swung the steering wheel all the way around, and the three-year-old Ford buckled insanely and flipped to the left, completely out of control.

The car landed in a cornfield, rolled over twice. The front and back windshields popped out. The side windows shattered to dust and blanketed him. He had cuts all over his face, glass sprinkled through his hair. His hands were bleeding and he had a pain in his stomach and he thought he was going to die, but the crash was over and somehow, God knew how, he had lived through it.

The door on his side was crushed and wouldn't open. The car was lying on that side and he couldn't climb out through the opposite door because he couldn't get to it. He went through the front window instead, crawled over the hood of the car, got off it and into the field.

He sat down, tried to rest for a moment. He had made it, somehow. He could get around, so that meant nothing was too badly broken. He might have some internal injuries, but if he did he didn't know what they were.

But someone was coming toward him. Someone would help him. He opened his mouth to call to the man, and only then did he notice that his teeth were broken and that blood was coming out of his mouth.

He stared at the man. He had never seen the man before. A tall, thin man, a man with a machine gun or something over one arm. A man who was pointing the gun at him.

"Sorry," the man was saying. "But no witnesses, huh?"

Then a stream of hot lead tore Luke Penner in half.

*　　　*　　　*

First they got the money out of the truck. That was no problem. Jimmy brought the Pontiac around, opened the trunk. McLeod hopped into the back of the truck and tossed out the sacks of money to Burl. Burl passed them to Lieber and Lieber stuffed them into the trunk.

Money was heavy, McLeod thought hysterically. Heavy money. Christ, maybe it was all a bunch of coins. A hundred thousand dollars in pennies.

He decided it wasn't possible. He kept lifting and tossing and then the truck was empty and he was on the ground again, running across to where Dawes was lying.

Dawes was alive, but barely. He had lost consciousness and he had done a lot of bleeding. McLeod sighed, put the barrel of his pistol to Dawes' head, and blew the man's brains out.

"We couldn't take him along," he told the others. "He had a few minutes, that's all. We couldn't get him to a hospital and we couldn't leave him to die later. Jesus, I had no choice."

"Forget it," Burl told him. Jimmy Kell nodded quickly. Mike Lieber gave him a funny look, then shrugged it off and got back into the Pontiac. McLeod wondered who the kid had been in the Ford. A crazy kid—he had plenty of room to get through, didn't have to go shooting off the road. Maybe he was trying to be a hero. Well, nobody was likely to give him a medal. Instead of a purple heart, Mike Lieber had stitched a row of bullet holes across his chest.

Jimmy had the engine going. He turned to Burl.

"Fast or slow?"

McLeod gave the answer. "Fast for five miles," he said. "Then slow and easy does it, and then we're home."

Jimmy nodded once. Then he let out the clutch and they were headed for Cedar Corners again.

They left the money in Burl's garage. The four of them unloaded it from the Pontiac. Jimmy wanted the car back, and nobody in the world could connect the convertible with the holdup. The car was clean so they let the kid have it back again. He was in a sweat, too, glad to be on his way. McLeod watched him go, then remembered why the kid was in such a rush.

He had a date.

A date to meet Betty Marie at the quarry. A date to celebrate the success of his job and the conclusion of her menstrual period.

A date with death.

McLeod chuckled.

"It went sweet," Burl was saying.

"Yeah."

"Except for Jack."

"I hated to do it, Burl. You know."

"I know."

"You think it was wrong?"

"Better that than letting him suffer, Marty."

"Sure," McLeod said. "That's the way I figured it."

"Well, now," Burl said. "I'll see you boys later."

The fat man walked to his door, went inside. McLeod's gun was in the waistband of his trousers again. He looked at Mike Lieber. Lieber had his chopper packed away in his guitar case and was holding the case by the handle. He looked more like an itinerant folksinger than a bandit.

How, McLeod wondered. Walk him home? Give him a ride home? It had to be a ride. Walking didn't make any sense, not when he had his car there.

"Come on," he said. "I'll give you a lift."

"I can walk."

"I'll drive you. Listen, we'll stop off at my place and have a few belts."

That would be better. Be tricky, getting to go up to Lieber's room. Trickier still trying to kill him without anyone hearing the shot. Take him for a ride, then kill him.

"I don't drink much," Lieber said.

"Just a quick one."

Lieber shrugged, got into the Chevy, set the guitar case across his knees. Just so it stays closed, McLeod thought. He walked around the car and got behind the wheel. He put the key in the slot, turned, started up.

He took the long way to the shack, then missed his cutoff on purpose. If he tried the play with the car in motion, Lieber could give him a tough time. He had to stop the car, and this gave him an excuse.

"The turn," Lieber said.

"I know. Hell."

He braked the car, slowed to a stop. He started the motion into reverse, then let go of the wheel and yanked the gun free from his belt. It was trained on Lieber's chest before the thin man could make a move.

For a long time Lieber didn't say a word. His eyes stayed on the gun, then moved up slowly to meet McLeod's. Lieber had very blue eyes, he noticed. He didn't look scared. He just seemed to be thinking, concentrating, looking for a way out.

McLeod said: "Get out of the car."

"Why should I?"

"Because otherwise you get it here. And if I have to do it that way I'll make it slow. I'll shoot you a few times, make it hurt a little. This way you at least get a quick death. That ought to be something."

"It's not very much."

"It's all you get."

Lieber took a long breath, let it out slowly. He opened his door and got out of the car. McLeod gave the guitar case a shove and watched it bounce onto the shoulder of the road. He crawled out across the seat, the gun still leveled at Lieber.

Lieber said: "Why?"

"Because I want all of it."

"All the money?"

"That's the idea."

"You can have it. You don't have to kill me to get it."

"It's a damn sight safer this way."

"Is it?"

"I think so."

Lieber nodded. "I thought you killed Dawes pretty

quick," he said. "I didn't want to say anything, figured it maybe was something personal. But that hole in his chest looked a hell of a lot more like a .38's work than any hole any chopper ever made. You timed it nice, though. I wasn't too sure, even with the hole to go by and the fact you shot him so quick later."

McLeod didn't say anything. Squeeze the trigger, he told himself. Don't talk shop with the bastard. Shoot him and go home, dammit. There are two more left.

"How about Burl and the kid?"

"What about them?"

"They in on this, too?"

"They're on your side," McLeod told him. "They get just what you're getting."

"I didn't figure Burl for a cross."

"He hasn't got the brains."

Lieber shrugged again. "You could have it all and I wouldn't be in your way. I'll just go home and mind my own business. I got a wife and kids, McLeod."

"So did some of those guards. We cut them up nice."

"You just don't care, do you?"

"Not a bit."

"Then what are you waiting for?"

The way to answer the question was with a burst of shots, but McLeod hesitated, fumbling for words. Then Mike Lieber forced the issue, charging at him, running at the mouth of the gun. McLeod gave the trigger a squeeze, heard a noise, watched Mike Lieber fall on his face.

The bullet took Lieber in the throat and tore a hole through his jugular vein. The blood poured out of him in a steady stream and McLeod watched, hypnotized, as the red fluid moved toward his own feet.

Blood.

He watched it, carefully. It was different, somehow, from how it had been before. He had killed once and had killed twice, and each time had been different.

The bank guard hardly counted at all. He had never met the bank guard, in the first place. And in the second place the bank guard was one of the enemy, a member of the other team. If he had not shot the guard, the guard would have gladly drilled a hole in McLeod's head instead.

So the bank guard didn't count.

And Jack? Jack counted, but not for much. The first shot had been during all the excitement, and Dawes was on the other side of the road at the time, and distance makes it easier. It is easier to send a guided missile toward a target than to shoot an enemy soldier in battle, and by the same token it is easier to shoot a man across the road than one a foot or two in front of you.

The second shot to Dawes? It was just a finishing touch. The man was virtually dead anyway.

But Lieber was different. He had been talking to Lieber. He had been close to Lieber, physically if not emotionally. And now Lieber's blood was almost licking his feet.

He took a quick step backward, shaking himself out of his reverie. He got into the Chevy, turned it around.

Burl and Jimmy were the only ones left. The girl was taking care of Jimmy.

That left Burl.

Chapter 11

When she heard the car, she took a deep breath and filled her lungs with air. She let the air out slowly. It had worked, then. They hadn't been killed, the job hadn't fallen flat on its face. Jimmy was on his way to her, and that meant that the job had gone off the way it was supposed to go off, that everything was all right, that McLeod was alive, that in an hour or so they would be on their way to a fresh new world.

She remembered Jimmy, and that she was going to kill him. She took the knife from her pocket, touched the blade for a second, then buried the knife up to the hilt in sand. She piled some gravel and sticks to conceal the hilt. He wouldn't see the knife, but it would be there when she wanted it.

The Pontiac convertible pulled up, braked to a stop. Jimmy tossed the door open, sprang from the car and ran to her. She had to force herself to register the right emotion. Somehow she managed it, going into her act instantly. She was on her feet, a smile of joy on her face. She ran to meet him and he caught her in his arms and fastened her mouth to his.

"You're all right," she said.

"Not a scratch."

"Thank God!"

He released her, took a step backward. "Some party," he said. "Some little shooting-match."

"How was it?"

"There's a driver and four guards on Route 147, and every last one of them is deader than hell."

She shivered. But it was more an act than a genuine emotion. She had taken the death of the guards for granted. That was part of the game.

"And," he said, "one of our men got it."

"Shot?"

"Dead."

She stiffened, and he was staring at her and she hardly cared. If McLeod was dead she didn't care about anything, about Jimmy, about the money, about herself.

If McLeod was dead—

"Who?" she demanded.

"Not me. So what's the difference?"

Asshole, she thought. It would be a pleasure to kill him, a genuine thrill to watch him die.

"Who was it?"

"A guy named Jack Dawes," he said. "What's the diff?"

She tried to relax without showing him that it made a very big difference to her. "I just wondered," she said.

"He caught a bullet and he was dying. Then McLeod finished him."

"Oh."

"Because we couldn't drag him with us," Jimmy went on. "The guy woulda croaked anyway."

She wanted to laugh. McLeod had killed him, all right. And that meant one less man for McLeod to kill in Cedar Corners. He had two to take care of, Lieber and Burl, and she had Jimmy to kill, and then they had nothing to worry about.

"Hey," he said.

She looked at him.

"You done?"

"Done what?"

"You know," he said. "The curse."

"I'm done."

"Well," he said. "I thought—I mean, I'm kind of keyed up after the job. And it's been a long time for us, Betty Marie. It's been too long. I need you, baby."

She let him take her in his arms, let him lead her to the side of the water. He kissed her. Slowly, very slowly, they sank to the ground.

She stretched out, drawing him on top of her. He was breathing hard and she knew just how much he wanted her, just how much he needed her. She reached back a hand, rubbed it along the sandy ground. She found the pile of sticks and gravel, brushed them away a little and touched the hilt of the knife.

All she had to do was lift and aim and stab. That was all. The knife would go in like a hot poker into a slab of butter and it would be all over for Jimmy. He didn't have a chance.

No, wait a sec . . .

A better idea. A beautiful, lovely, absolutely delicious sort of an idea. A charmer.

She wrapped her arms around him, kissed him hard. His lips parted and her warm tongue danced between them, stroking the inside of his mouth, lighting little fires wherever it landed. The passion was not entirely put on now. She was hot, not for him but for the act and the denouement she was planning. She was passionate, burning, aching.

"My breasts," she said.

His hands found them, held them. He began to knead her breasts, then stopped long enough to get her blouse open. She was not wearing a bra. He stopped for a moment, gasped at the sight of the huge round globes of flesh. Then he was holding her bare breasts, fondling them, pinching and pulling at the firm nipples. Sweat poured from his brow. He was all excited, and she could feel how much he wanted her.

"Take off my clothes," she said.

He took off her clothes, then his own. He took off everything, and his hands explored the full rich curves of her hot young body, and his mouth moved to her breast.

There was something tremendously exciting about it. He was making love to her, kissing and tonguing her breasts, and in a few moments he was going to die.

She was going to kill him.

This, all by itself, was exciting. Both factors were exciting, and when you put them both together they spelled delirium, and she was delirious already. She put one hand on the back of his head, stroking his hair while he kissed her breast, and she put the other hand on the hilt of the knife.

No.

Not just yet.

There was no reason to stop. Let it get as good as it could, as exciting as possible.

Let the world fly.

Let the sun sing.

He had his hand on her thigh now. He moved the hand upward, found her, stroked her. He was still kissing her breasts, running a warm tongue over the stiff nipples, and he was touching her with hot fingers, poking and probing and fanning the flames of her mad desire.

Then he was ready.

He moved forward, put his mouth to hers. His chest was crushing her breasts and his being was touching her, ready to enter her. He was ready, and he was about to make love to her, and she, too, was ready.

She reached back.

Her hand closed around the hilt of the knife. She tugged it free of the sand, reversed it in her hand. He was too busy to notice, too engrossed in what he was doing to pay any attention to the knife. She moved it, held it so that the tip of the blade was poised a few inches above the center of his back.

And then he was inside her, moving madly within her, his whole body shaking and stabbing spasmodically. She felt his passion mount, and she looked up into his eyes, eyes that were wild with lust.

Now!

She drove the knife down, down into his back, down straight for his heart. The blade sank in smoothly, sank in all the way, and she felt him quiver with pain, and she looked into his eyes and watched him die.

It didn't take him very long. His eyes were wide at first, wide with pain and fear and total shock, and then his eyes glazed over and the light went out of them, and his head fell forward, and the man between her thighs, the man whose dick was still inside her, was dead.

Her hips churned for a few moments. She was hot as a firecracker, and she used the dead body of Jimmy Kell to finish what the live body had started. At last she shook and heaved with a fulfillment in which he was unable to participate. Then she lay for a second or two, exhausted.

Finally she pushed his corpse off her, struggled to her feet. She looked at him. There had been very little bleeding. The wound was a clean one and the blade had found his heart. She got her hands on a cigarette, lit it. She smoked it all the way down and buried the butt in the sand.

The sun was hot on her bare body, but she did not get dressed right away. First she dragged Jimmy's corpse to the water's edge, pushing him in and giving him enough of a shove to send him out a ways toward the middle. He sank below the surface and out of sight. In time the gases in his body, gases created by the decomposition of his flesh, would bring him to the surface. But for the time being no one was likely to stumble over him.

She slipped into the water herself, washing blood and

the smell of sex from her body. She got out, dried herself off with Jimmy's clothes. Then she tossed them into the trunk of the Pontiac and put on her own clothes. He had left the keys in the car. She drove it around a bend, parked it between two rows of poplars. Somebody would find it just as somebody would find Jimmy. But not right away.

She started a fresh cigarette. The knife, its blade bloody, was still at her feet. She picked it up by the hilt and looked at it. Fingerprints? That was silly. If they were caught it was all over and fingerprints were not going to make any difference. She threw the knife into the middle of the quarry and watched it go to the bottom.

Jimmy had worried her. Telling her one of the gang was dead, then not letting her know at first who it was. It could have been McLeod.

God!

She started shaking all over again. No, she thought, it wasn't McLeod. McLeod was her man, and she loved him and he loved her, and soon he would be coming for her.

Joyce had been awake when Burl got home. He got rid of the rest of them, then went inside, and there she was. She was sipping coffee. He took the cup away from her and smelled it. She had laced it with shine.

She looked at him. "Where's your friend?"

Dead, he thought. Instead he told her that Dawes had left town, that something had come up and he couldn't make it back. He was sorry, he went on, but that was the way it was.

"Nice guy," Joyce said. "Didn't even say goodbye."

"Well, now. It was sudden, you know."

"He have a good time last night?"

"You ought to know better than me."

She winked at him. "Should not," she said. "You had a better view than I did, wise guy. Have a good eyeful?"

He nodded.

"Shame he's not here. You could do some more watching, Burl. I feel like going a round or two."

He felt it himself. It was understandable, a strong sexual need after the completion of a dangerous job of one sort or another. You risked death, and afterward you were alive, and sexual union was a sort of reaffirmation of that life that seemed so precious all of a sudden.

"Maybe we don't need him," he said slowly.

"No?"

"Maybe I could take his place, Joyce."

She arched an eyebrow. "You? I thought you were just a watchbird, Burl."

"Usually."

"What else do you do?"

"I don't do much," he said after a moment. "I usually get done to."

She didn't understand. He raised one hand, extended one finger, put it to her lips.

"Oh," she said.

He didn't say anything.

"All right," she said.

"All right?"

"Sure," she said recklessly. "Why the hell not, Burl? What have I got to lose?"

"Well, now," he said.

He took her by the arm and led her to the bedroom, the same room where she and Dawes had made love the night before. That might help, he thought. He could sit there with his eyes closed and imagine he was watching them again. They had put on one hell of a good show, Joyce and Dawes. Just running that show through his mind ought to be enough.

In the bedroom, he took off all his clothes. She started to strip down, then stopped and asked him whether she should get undressed or not. It didn't really matter much, but he decided she'd like it better that way. He told her to undress and she did.

A good body, he saw. The body Dawes had used so magnificently. He sat down on the edge of the bed, remembering, and she sank to her knees before him.

The door wasn't locked. McLeod gave it a shove and it flew open. He put his hand on the butt of the gun, stepped over the threshold. The room was empty.

Come out, he thought evenly. *Come out, come out wherever you are. Come out and die.*

He looked around the room. There was an afghan on

the couch, and he went to it and picked it up. He folded it small, then drew the gun and wrapped the afghan around it. That would solve one problem. The afghan would make a fairly effective silencer. It would muffle the noise of the gunshot enough to prevent a neighbor from hearing it.

"Burl!" he called.

There was no answer.

He swore. The son of a bitch had to be home; otherwise everything was all off schedule. Or suppose Burl had skipped with all of the money—that would be cute, wouldn't it? He'd have nothing at all, not a pot to piss in, and he'd be wanted for too many murders.

He thought of Betty Marie, waiting for him at the quarry. He had to get Burl, had to get that money, had to pick up the girl and get the hell out of Indiana.

"Burl!"

Silence, for a moment.

Then: "Don't come in!"

For a moment he thought Burl was afraid. Somehow Burl knew he was after him, and Burl was telling him to stay away. But that didn't make any sense at all. Burl hadn't seemed to be suspecting a double-cross at all, hadn't noticed a thing when he shot Dawes and then finished him off.

He thought a moment. Burl was in the bedroom; that was where the sound had come from. Maybe Burl had a broad with him, maybe he was balling somebody.

There couldn't be a better time.

He took off his shoes, padded noiselessly across the floor in his socks. He walked down the hallway to the bedroom.

The door was closed. He held the gun, wrapped in the afghan, in his right hand. He took the doorknob with his left, turned it slowly, then shoved the door open.

For a moment he simply stared. Burl was on the bed, eyes open now, panting. Joyce Ramsdell was on the floor in front of him facing Burl.

He stared, but only briefly.

Then he fired.

The bullet went into Burl's mouth. Burl's mouth was open at the time, and the bullet sailed in and went out through the back of Burl's head without stopping to say hello. The gunshot was a dry cough muffled by the afghan. Burl was on his back, tossed over by the force of the gunshot, and he was dead before what was left of his head hit the bedspread.

Joyce turned and screamed.

The scream didn't last very long. McLeod kicked her in the mouth, and that shut her up. He steadied the gun, aimed it at her. Her mouth was open again but she wasn't screaming. She was looking up at him and she looked scared to death. He knew what it was. The broad was too scared to scream. She couldn't move a muscle, couldn't make a sound.

"You stupid tramp," he said.

She didn't say anything.

"You had to be here," he went on. "You stupid tramp, you had to be here, you had to pick this time to go down on that fat old slob. You never get enough, do you? You take anything you can get, and now I have to kill you."

She tried to get to her feet. She didn't make it and she wound up on her knees again, looking up at him.

"You had to be a witness," he said. "Dammit, you really walked into one, you moron."

He squeezed the trigger. The hammer clicked on nothing. The gun was empty, and he looked at it for a moment, then stuck it into his pocket.

He didn't need a gun.

He killed her with his bare hands. When he touched her throat she tried to struggle, but it didn't do her any good. He was too strong for her. He wrapped his big hands around her neck and he squeezed, and a vein stood out on her forehead and her eyes bulged halfway out of her head, and he squeezed harder and harder with all his strength until finally something had to give.

Her neck gave. She went limp in his hands and her head fell forward, and when he took her pulse he found out that she was dead.

Funny. He got a hard-on strangling her, feeling her struggling within his grip. He didn't want her, didn't really want to have sex, but his dick had a mind of its own. He went to the sink, got a glass of water, drank it down, filled it and drank again. And stood there, waiting, while his curious passion cooled.

The money was in the garage, all of it. He looked through one of the sacks, just giving it a quick check, and he knew that there was a lot of money there, a tremendous amount of it. He had no idea how much it was and he didn't care to find out. There would be time to count it. This wasn't the time.

He backed the Chevy up to the garage and filled the trunk with the sacks of money. The car had a smaller trunk than the Pontiac and he had to junk the spare in order to make room for the dough. It didn't matter. He wouldn't need the spare. They figured to use a lot of cars between Indiana and Mexico, and all the tires would still be functioning when he got rid of the Chevy and picked up a fresh car off the streets.

He got behind the wheel. He filled the .38 with a batch of shells and stuck it in the glove compartment. Betty Marie was waiting for him, and he wanted to get to her in a hurry.

He drove fast, pushing the Chevy hard. He took the cut-off to the quarry, put the accelerator all the way down and went in fast. He braked hard when he spotted her and she came running to meet him, throwing open his door and leaping into his arms.

"God," she said.

He asked her how it went.

"All right," she said. "I knew I could do it, McLeod, but it was almost too easy. I put the knife in him and he died. Just one stab and he was dead. It was the easiest thing in the world."

Easy, he thought. It seemed as though there was nothing

in the world quite so easy as killing a man. You could do it in the dark with your eyes closed. You could do it any time at all, and you could shrug it off as soon as you were through, and that was all there was to it.

"Come on," he said. "We'd better get going."

"Now?"

"Now."

"I wish we could make love first, McLeod."

"No time, baby."

"You're right," she said. "You're right. They'll be after us, won't they?"

"Sooner or later."

"Will they catch us?"

"I don't know."

She nodded quickly, then ran around the car and got in on her side. She slammed the door shut and he started the car again, turned it around, drove away from the quarry.

"I thought . . . I thought you were dead," she said.

"Why?"

"Jimmy told me someone from the gang was killed. I thought it was you for a minute."

"It was Dawes. I shot him there."

"That's what I figured. Was it hard, McLeod?"

Was it hard? He thought it over, thinking and driving at the same time. He pushed the Chevy, got out of Cedar Corners and on the way to the state line. Was it hard? Were any of them hard? Was Dawes hard? Was Lieber hard? Was Burl hard, or Joyce? Was the job hard?

"It wasn't hard." he said at last.

"Not at all?"

"Not at all," he said. "It was all easy, start to finish. Too easy, maybe. So easy it scares me."

She opened her mouth, then closed it. She kept it shut from then on and let him concentrate on the driving.

Chapter 12

And they lived happily ever after.

They didn't, of course. And wouldn't it be terrible if they did? Think it over for a moment. Suppose Betty Marie James and Martin McLeod *did* live happily ever after, or as close as possible. Say they got to Mexico, and they found a place to live, and they were married, and they had children, and they lived a high old life until they both died in their sleep fifty years later.

Wouldn't that be disappointing?

Of course it would. There's a tremendous amount of satisfaction in seeing someone tripped up when they have done wrong, and no one more assuredly did wrong than this happy couple. So it would be a fictive catastrophe if they lived happily ever after, and we would all promptly go into a state of traumatic shock, each and every one of us.

Well, don't worry about it. They did not live happily ever after, thank the Lord.

This is what happened:

*   *   *

They cut across the Illinois line, knifed down through southern Illinois to the Mississippi. McLeod drove the Chevy onto a ferry crossing the river to Missouri. There they spent the night at a motel. The name of the motel was The Friendly Motel, and the proprietor was an outgoing ready-to-please bumpkin who wanted to be friendly. McLeod got rid of him, told him to bring a bottle of bourbon and a bucket of ice and go away. The man brought the liquor and the ice and took McLeod's money and went away.

"Take a breath," he told Betty Marie. "There's all of Illinois between us and them. Drink?"

"I think I could use one."

He opened the bottle, put ice in the glasses, poured liquor over the ice cubes. He asked her if she wanted water with hers. She didn't. He handed her a glass, touched glasses with her, and drank.

"I gave him phony names," he said. "Plus wrong license plate numbers. I switched a few digits around."

"Won't he get suspicious?"

"Everybody does it," he said. "Whenever you're making somebody's wife in a motel you give phony everything. He's too busy being everyman's friend to notice, anyway. Drink up."

He worked on his own drink, then made a fresh one. He felt funny, much tighter inside than before when he had been doing all the planning and all the killing. He tried to figure out why it was. One reason came to him right away.

"We're running," he said.

She looked at him.

"We're running. We're on the lam."

"Of course. So what?"

"So that's why I don't feel the same," he said. "I was cooler before. I was doing the chasing then and everybody else was running, trying to stay alive. I was the aggressor. You get what I'm driving at?"

"A little."

He nodded. "Now we're the ones who are running, whether or not anybody's trying to catch us. It's a completely different feeling. We stood a bigger chance of getting killed before but it didn't matter. I wasn't worried about it at all then. I didn't even think about dying. Did you?"

"No."

"I think about it now," he said. "We're safer now, and we stand a better chance, and I think about it. I suppose I'm afraid, kitten."

"I don't think you're afraid of anything in the world."

He shrugged. Suddenly he remembered a different world, a world where he was a young lawyer living in a mortgaged house and married to a woman he loved at the time. He had worried then. Worried about cases, about money. Little worries when you measured them against the fear of death. Well, that was the whole point, wasn't it? He was playing in a different league.

"There's a radio," he said. "You get an hour for twenty-five cents. You believe it? This shithole is fancy enough to have a radio and cheap enough to charge you to use it. Got a quarter?"

"I don't want to hear music."

"To hell with music. There might be something about the deal. We could get some idea of where they're looking for us."

She dug out a quarter and handed it to him. He played the radio, tried to find a newscast. It took him fifteen minutes before he caught one and it didn't tell him much. There was a report of the hold-up, of course. There was nothing about the murders in Cedar Corners.

"They can't be onto us yet," he said. "They haven't made the connection. As soon as they find the dead bodies in Cedar Corners and put two and two together, then they'll be on our trail. But by that time we'll be farther away."

"We'll make it," she said.

"Yeah."

"We will, won't we?"

"I think so," he said. "I think we will."

He had another drink, a stiff one. Then they undressed and got into bed. Her flesh was warm, soft. He took her in his arms and kissed her, and when his mouth met hers her whole body started to shake. At first he mistook the trembling for passion and he was about to tell her she had the shortest fuse in creation. Then he realized why she was shaking.

She was scared, too.

That helped a little. It was no good thinking you were the only frightened passenger on the airplane, because then you inevitably felt that somehow you had been gifted with inside information, that the plane was an odds-on bet to crash and the others were foolishly over-confident. But this way with her sharing his fears, it was somehow more tolerable all around, more easy to bear.

"Easy," he said. "Easy."

"McLeod—"

"Steady, kitten."

He petted her, stroked her. There was nothing particularly sensual about the caresses he gave her. He was trying to make her relax, not to heat her up. He held her breasts in his big hands, ran his hands over her belly, her thighs.

He kissed her, and she clutched him feverishly, holding him to keep him and the world from getting away from her. He kissed her eyelids, one and then the other, and he kissed the hollow of her throat.

"My little girl," he said.

"A big girl."

"Sure. A woman."

"You love me, don't you?"

"I love you, kitten."

"And I love you, McLeod. No matter . . . no matter what happens, I love you. And I'm glad."

"Uh-huh."

"Make . . . make love to me, McLeod."

The love they made was unlike anything they had ever experienced before. It was not especially passionate. Instead, it was soft, gentle, slow, yielding. They were seeking each other and finding each other, reaching each other and touching each other.

Comforting each other.

And, at the end, when their bodies shuddered together at the culmination, it was still more need than lust, more emotional than physical.

She cried, afterward. He didn't, but he wished he was able to. It would have been good to cry right about then.

He caught another 25¢ newscast in the morning before they left, and evidently they had made a lot of progress during the night. They had found Burl and Joyce, and they had found Jimmy's car and were dredging for Jimmy. They'd found Mike Lieber.

They had also found someone named Susan Craig, who had apparently been hanged in her bedroom. He wasn't sure how the hell she fit into everything, but it would be one more murder charge to be thrown at them. It was time to roll, time to get to Mexico.

They had breakfast in a roadside diner and traded cars with somebody from Nebraska on the way out. McLeod jumped the ignition and started the car without a key while Betty Marie followed him for half a mile in the Chevy. They switched the money from one trunk to the other and McLeod ran the Chevy off the road into a culvert. Then they were on the road again in the new car, on the road and heading south. The new car was an Olds, anonymously dark, a big sedan with a big engine. It had power steering and power brakes and power windows and power seats, and it also surprisingly enough, had some power left over that was directed to the engine. McLeod hugged the western bank of the Mississippi and drove due south.

It was better in the daylight, with the car moving. It had been hell at night, because then they had been standing still and the consequent feeling of impotence was terrible. They were running, and there is nothing worse than waiting between sprints when you are running for your life. You get the feeling that you ought to be doing something, that you're not getting anywhere and the world is closing in.

The Olds had a radio, naturally. They were almost through Kansas when he caught the stolen car report and heard the Olds identified as their current car.

"That didn't take them long," he said. "Guy reported it stolen and they went out and spotted the Chevy and put two and two together. Now every cop in six states knows what car to look for."

"What do we do now?"

"We get a new car," he told her.

They bought the new one. They hit a small town in southern Kansas near the Oklahoma line, and Betty Marie stayed in the Olds while McLeod looked for an auto dealer who wouldn't let principles get in the way of a pretty profit. McLeod had to trade even, giving him the Olds for an old Plymouth.

"Once you're riding high," he said, "then every jerk in the world has his hand out."

"At least the car's safe."

"Yeah," he said. "He can't report us or he's in hot water himself. That has to be something."

It was something, but it wasn't enough.

From the beginning they never stood a chance. It's too far from Indiana to Mexico, for one thing. A plane would have done it, but when you're three days of hard driving away from your destination you give the law time to get there first. They hadn't had a plane, and the news got out too fast, and they never really had a chance at all.

They were lucky to get as far as they did. McLeod left the Mississippi to cut through Kansas on a slant, and by doing this he dodged a roadblock without knowing it. The law figured he would break for Mexico, and they'd had a fragmentary report on him, and there was a block set up on the road he was taking. But he missed that one, and he was lucky.

Luck only holds so far. Sooner or later it runs out on you, and when it runs out you get your turn at the other end of the stick. Their turn came that night, in Oklahoma.

The next stop after Oklahoma was supposed to be Texas. Then they were supposed to layover in a motel or a cabin for the night and make Mexico the following day. McLeod didn't figure on much trouble at the border. It was a problem he would solve when he came to it.

He never came to it. They never got past Oklahoma.

He saw the first roadblock. He saw cars stopped ahead of him, and he smelled police, and he peeled off onto a dirt road and put the gas pedal on the floor. The dirt road widened, and then it branched into another road, and he cut left without knowing where it led. It didn't really matter where it was going. Because he heard a siren open up behind him, and he prayed to God that the Plymouth would show enough guts to beat the trooper who was on his tail, and at the same time he prayed that the road he was on would go somewhere worthwhile.

It didn't.

It went to a roadblock.

This one seemed to open up in front of him, and all at once he knew how the kid had felt, the one who went off the road during the robbery, the one Lieber gunned down. He felt that way now; there was a wall in front of him with no way around it and he was coming at it at better than eighty-five miles an hour, and they had him trapped like a rat.

Betty Marie was clutching his arm, her nails digging through his shirt and into his skin. She was saying his name over and over, screaming it, chanting it.

"We'll shoot right through it," he said.

"Good."

Neither of them believed it. He kept the pedal on the floor, praying, praying to God, wondering why God should listen to him, wondering what was going to happen when he died. He had all that money in the trunk and he was never going to spend it and it was all over, all but the shouting.

They hit the block at what was probably its weakest point. Two patrol cars were parked facing one another, nose to nose, and McLeod drove the Plymouth at top speed into the two noses. The impact was tremendous, and for the shadow of a second he thought that it had worked, that God had been listening to him, that they were going to make it.

He was wrong.

The Plymouth buckled and collapsed in on itself, with the back of the car and the front of the car inches apart. Betty Marie James went through the windshield before it broke. The Medical Examiner decided that the fall had killed her, because she was thrown forty yards and landed on the base of her spine. But if the fall hadn't killed her she wouldn't have lived anyway. They couldn't find very much of her face when they came around to shovel her up.

McLeod died in the car. The steering wheel went through his chest, and round after round of bullets went into the rest of him, and he died.

The wreckers came for the Plymouth. They swept up the shattered glass and the hunks of steel, and they towed the car and the two cop cars to the junkyard. They sponged blood off the road and shipped most of McLeod and most of Betty Marie to Indiana for burial. The world took a breath and relaxed, and the town of Cedar Corners settled back and waited for something else to happen.

My Newsletter: I get out an email newsletter at unpredictable intervals, but rarely more often than every other week. I'll be happy to add you to the distribution list. A blank email to lawbloc@gmail.com with "newsletter" in the subject line will get you on the list, and a click of the "Unsubscribe" link will get you off it, should you ultimately decide you're happier without it.

About the Author

Lawrence Block has been writing award-winning mystery and suspense fiction for half a century. His newest book, a sequel to his greatly successful Hopper anthology *In Sunlight or in Shadow*, is *Alive in Shape and Color*, a 17-story anthology with each story illustrated by a great painting; authors include Lee Child, Joyce Carol Oates, Michael Connelly, Joe Lansdale, Jeffery Deaver and David Morrell. His most recent novel, pitched by his Hollywood agent as "James M. Cain on Viagra," is *The Girl with the Deep Blue Eyes*. Other recent works of fiction include *The Burglar Who Counted The Spoons*, featuring Bernie Rhodenbarr; *Keller's Fedora*, featuring philatelist and assassin Keller; and *A Drop Of The Hard Stuff*, featuring Matthew Scudder, brilliantly embodied by Liam Neeson in the 2014 film, *A Walk Among The Tombstones*. Several of his other books have also been filmed, although not terribly well. He's well known for his books for writers, including the classic *Telling Lies For Fun & Profit* and *Write For Your Life*, and has recently published a collection of his writings about the mystery genre and its practitioners, *The Crime Of Our Lives*. In addition to prose works, he has written episodic television (*Tilt!*) and the Wong Kar-wai film, *My Blueberry Nights*. He is a modest and humble fellow, although you would never guess as much from this biographical note.

Email: lawbloc@gmail.com
Twitter:@LawrenceBlock
Facebook: lawrence.block
Website: lawrenceblock.com